Ellie was awa
shyness.

Now she knew there was no one in the world more worthy of respect. And her new respect was even tinged with a little awe.

The smile still lurked in Dr Carmody's eyes as he brought his cup of tea to her desk and arranged his powerful form beside her in a chair, and Ellie knew the urge to study this enigmatic man anew.

Dear Reader

Autumn books to warm the heart! Gideon really believes he has NOTHING LEFT TO GIVE until Beth proves him wrong, in Caroline Anderson's latest story. Their past relationship makes Alison and Grant decide to be STRICTLY PROFESSIONAL in work, according to Laura MacDonald. Abigail Gordon's CALMER WATERS and Judith Ansell's HIS SHELTERING ARMS are equally touching. We think you'll love these stories.

The Editor

!!!STOP PRESS!!! If you enjoy reading these medical books, have you ever thought of writing one? We are always looking for new writers for LOVE ON CALL, and want to hear from you. Send for the guidelines, with SAE, and start writing!

Judith Ansell is a doctor who has always had an interest in writing. She has worked in many different and sometimes exciting areas of medicine, and thus has an excellent background for writing medical stories. At present she combines part-time medical practice with writing, and caring for her unruly child. She is married to a surgeon, and can affirm that doctors make excellent and patient husbands.

Recent titles by the same author:

HEARTS OUT OF TIME
THE CONSTANT HEART
A SPECIAL CHALLENGE

HIS SHELTERING ARMS

BY
JUDITH ANSELL

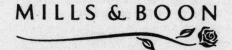

MILLS & BOON

MILLS & BOON LIMITED
ETON HOUSE, 18–24 PARADISE ROAD
RICHMOND, SURREY, TW9 1SR

MILLS & BOON, the Rose Device and LOVE ON CALL are trademarks of the publisher.

First published in Great Britain 1994 by Mills & Boon Limited

© Judith Ansell 1994

Australian copyright 1994   Philippine copyright 1994 This edition 1994

ISBN 0 263 78828 8

Set in 10 on 11½ pt Linotron Times 03-9410-62674

Typeset in Great Britain by Centracet, Cambridge Made and printed in Great Britain

CHAPTER ONE

ELINOR STANDISH slid from the seat of her car and stood gazing for a moment at the collection of buildings which made up Berringar Base Hospital. She was tense — uncomfortably so, and torn between joy at having been offered the coming interview and a craven desire to turn tail and make off down the same road she had travelled to arrive here. For it seemed to Ellie vastly unlikely that someone as inexperienced as she could possibly be given the job of sister in charge of Casualty. She had completed her nursing degree only three years ago, and jobs like this attracted competition. Berringar Base was only a small country hospital, but it had a reputation for excellence, and its setting on the far south coast of New South Wales, between dazzling white beaches and mountain forests, couldn't be beaten.

Ellie took a slow, deep breath and brushed a wrinkle from her skirt. She had never been for an interview before, having trained and worked at the one giant hospital in Sydney. She had debated long about whether to wear her uniform, but had decided against it. She looked older in 'civvies'. Hoping that her crisp white shirt and dark blue gabardine skirt gave her the right air of neatness and efficiency, she squared her shoulders and trod towards the main building.

At the sound of the approaching car, Dr Paul Vassy, surgeon, had sauntered out on to the side-veranda of the old hospital building which now served jointly as admin block and staff quarters, and had been able to observe the arrival of the last applicant for the post of casualty sister.

'*Tiens*!' he uttered, surprised into his native language for a moment by what he saw. For the young woman who emerged from the rather battered four-wheel drive was not what he had been expecting, and nothing like any of the previous ones. She was of medium height, rather slim, which perhaps made her look taller than she was. Her form was gracefully curved despite the slimness. She had a rather athletic look.

As she approached the graceful old building he had the opportunity for closer inspection, and Ellie's confidence would hardly have been augmented by his conclusion. She was impossibly young. She had glossy, honey-coloured hair, hanging straight to just above her shoulders. Her eyes were a lovely and rather unusual green. Her face was further endowed with a classical little nose and a pair of most enchanting lips, the upper of which was shorter than the lower and not as full, which gave her the appearance of being about to break into an impish smile. She could, Paul concluded, have been a fashion model.

The interview had been a fiasco, Ellie decided. She had driven away down the road again and through the town of Berringar without really knowing what she was doing, and had pulled up now at one of the look-outs on the road to the coast. She stood at the edge of the look-out, a panorama of undulating eucalypt forest before her, and in the far distance the blue gleam of the sea. A cool coastal breeze fanned her still flushed cheeks and consoled her just a little.

It was not that they hadn't been kind, she thought. Paul Vassy, the Frenchman, and the large vague man

who was the medical superintendent had been very
pleasant and had encouraged her, she felt, to present
at her best. Matron, though formidable, had listened
politely as Ellie had explained why she wanted to work
at Berringar, and why she thought she could do the
job. The other man, the good-looking one, Simon
Taverner—she wasn't so sure about him. He had been
friendly enough, but he had a vaguely mocking, patronising air that she didn't like.

It was just that she had been hopeless, she thought,
mentally lashing herself. She had stammered and stumbled and misunderstood their questions. Not that any
of them had been unexpected—it was just that the
answers she had intended to give, which indeed she
had rehearsed in her mind so many times, had seemed
somehow inadequate beneath Matron's steely gaze and
Dr Taverner's faintly satirical one. It had somehow
reduced her to a state of complete ineptitude so
different from her usual calm competence that she
couldn't understand what had happened to her. The
only brief return of Ellie's customary adroitness had
occurred when the large man next to her, the super,
had pushed his coffee-cup too near the edge of the arm
of his chair, and she had in one swift movement caught
it as it fell.

And now that the first flush of embarrassment had
passed, Ellie felt the sharper pangs of disappointment
and dismay. For they wouldn't give her the job. She
was sure of that. She had shown herself too clearly for
what she was—a totally inexperienced girl, still wet
behind the ears.

Had Ellie been privileged to hear the discussion of her
that followed the interview, it would have been little

comfort but no surprise to hear how closely Matron's sentiments echoed her own.

'Three years isn't much experience for a positon like this,' Matron Fowler observed. 'She's only twenty-five.' Grace Fowler and the three senior doctors sat in the same room that had witnessed the interview, the room that was generally used as a common-room for the doctors and sisters who lived in the quarters.

The large man, Charles Carmody, had once again a cup of coffee balanced perilously on the wooden arm of his chair, and appeared to be contemplating the pattern of the carpet absently.

Simon Taverner lounged in his chair with his legs crossed at the ankles. He was, as Ellie had noted, a good-looking man, of average height and a lithe, athletic frame. His dark blond hair curled attractively and his deep blue eyes were set in a tanned face with good regular features, though the mouth was perhaps a little small and womanish. There was, in repose, a lazy, sardonic look to him, but when he smiled he was singularly charming. He was twenty-nine, and was the physician at Berringar, in charge of the medical patients.

Paul Vassy, who had somehow found his way to this spot from Rouen, was physically and temperamentally a contrast to him. He was thirty-four—the same age as the med super. But Paul was short, dark and wiry, with an expressive face and quick, emphatic movements. He was a quick-tempered man, often rather critical, but he could also be sympathetic and shrewdly observant.

'She's got her cas certificate. And her references are excellent. They obviously think a lot of her at North Shore,' Taverner was saying.

'Yes, they are very good,' Paul Vassy answered.

'And she is a pleasant young woman. She will try hard to fit in.' He turned to Matron Fowler. 'That is very important here, yes? It is a small place. We work and eat and live together.'

'Yes, Dr Vassy. I do appreciate that. Our most experienced applicant — Sister Blundell — may be a little — er — forceful, perhaps.'

Paul rolled his eyes. 'But yes! Please, not that one!' He shrugged. 'She is very young, this one. But not at all stupid, I think.'

Taverner flicked his blue eyes up. 'And she does have the certificate. And North Shore is a very busy cas. She may have had more experience in terms of patient numbers than some of the older ones.'

Paul Vassy agreed. 'Yes. For me, this little one or that MacMurtagh woman. The girl, for choice. I cannot pronounce that one's name.'

Taverner laughed, showing even white teeth. 'Not perhaps the best reason for choosing her.' He turned to the third man, who had so far been wrapped in a contemplative silence that was common to him. 'Charlie — what do you think?'

The large man looked as though he had been thinking of something entirely different, which might well have been the case. He gave a genial if vague smile. 'Oh, whatever you think,' he said. 'I'm sure they're all very good.' And, seeing a measure of impatience in his colleagues' faces and the expectation that he would say more, added, 'Very quick, that girl. Caught my cup before it hit the ground.'

The offer of the job, when it came, amazed Ellie. She wondered what the other applicants could have been like, if they considered her the best of them, and remarked on it to her mother. That stalwart champion of all her children could not be brought to agree, however.

'I'm sure they've chosen very wisely,' she asserted. 'You'll do a wonderful job, darling, just as you always do.'

Ellie grinned at her mother in fond amusement. 'How wonderful it is to have one person in the world in the eyes of whom one can do no wrong!' she said.

Mrs Standish gave a little chuckle. 'Well, now, Ellie, I never said that. I remember a few incidents. . .'

Ellie laughed. 'Oh, no! Don't remind me of my childhood sins!'

'Well,' smiled Mrs Standish, 'they weren't so very bad. And I know you'll be wonderful. I only wish you had a little more confidence in yourself, Ellie.'

'Oh, when I'm with patients I'm confident enough. It's just that it's hard to believe they could want me when they had so many to choose from.'

'Yes. You were always like that,' her mother observed. 'A nice, modest little girl who got along with everyone.'

'I hope I can get along with everyone at Berringar,' Ellie remarked. 'It's a dream come true to be working there, with the sea half an hour's drive in one direction and the national park about the same in the other.'

'Don't you get lost in the national park, Ellie,' Mrs Standish cautioned her outdoorsy daughter.

Ellie laughed. 'With all the walking and climbing and camping I've done, have I ever got lost?'

'And watch out for bushfires,' advised her mother, busily imagining all the evils that could possibly overtake her child.

'And snakes, and wild pigs, and bunyips,' Ellie promised, the solemnity of her tone belied by the laughter in her eyes and the upturned corners of her mouth.

Ellie's little Suzuki four-wheeled drive was groaning as it left the town of Berringar behind and crawled up the hill towards the hospital. The Base, as it was known, squatted in the foothills of the ranges that rose behind the town, only five minutes' drive from the town centre, but separated from it by a few miles of farmland. More farms spread away to the north and south of it, and behind reared the abrupt and rugged mountains of the Goolcoola National Park. The back compartment of the Suzuki, and even the passenger seat, was packed with gear—clothes, camping equipment, books, even a few pictures to hang on the walls of the quarters which were to be Ellie's home for at least, she hoped, the next few years. Gaining the rise at last, she changed up through the gears, and her heart seemed to swell as she caught a glimpse through the trees of the district the hospital served, of sunlit fertile plains below them and the snug little town in the centre.

She turned in at last through the hospital gates and followed the curved drive to the quarters. There she drew up in the car park and climbed gratefully out of the Suzuki. It was a wonderful vehicle to do the things she liked to do in her spare time, but on a long trip it was noisy and jarring. Ellie set out to tell someone she was here and to find her room, then was brought up short as she rounded the corner of the building to see the med super, Dr Carmody, squatting on his heels on the lawn in the dying sunlight. Around him was gathered a small mob of grey kangaroos, vying with each other to take his bread.

Ellie approached softly, but the shy animals heard her and stood suddenly as immobile as statues, their sensitive faces lifted in her direction, sniffing the air. Then, as though at a signal, the whole mob wheeled at once, breaking into their preposterous bounding stride and covering the distance to the trees in moments.

'Oh, I'm sorry!' exclaimed Ellie as Dr Carmody uncoiled himself and rose to a more impressive height than Ellie had remembered. 'I didn't mean to frighten them away. I thought they must be used to humans.'

But Dr Carmody seemed to be more apologetic than angry. 'Well, no — not really. That is — they're used to me,' he said with a wry smile, then explained, 'I'm the only one who feeds them. But they'd soon grow used to anyone who offered them food and didn't hurt them.'

Ellie smiled shyly in return. 'Will they come back?'

'Oh, yes.' The big man nodded.

Ellie noticed the same air of vagueness about him that she had noted at her interview, and wondered suddenly if he remembered who she was. Should she tell him? But before she could decide he murmured, 'Here they come,' and handed her a piece of bread. So it was that Ellie found herself on her first afternoon at the Base squatting on the lawn beside the crouching bulk of the medical superintendent, feeding bread to a mob of kangaroos, who quickly seemed to decide that any friend of Dr Carmody's was a friend of theirs.

'It's different from Royal North Shore Hospital!' Ellie remarked when they had finished, as much to remind him of who she was as anything.

Dr Carmody smiled down benignly out of a face that conveyed an impression of good-humoured kindness. 'Yes,' he answered, and ran a hand through rather tousled brown hair. 'Now, I wonder what we ought to do with you?' he said uncertainly. 'Perhaps Matron. . .'

Ellie was cheered to see that at least he had recollected who she was and why she was there.

'Perhaps someone can show me where my room is, and I can unpack,' she suggested gently.

He brightened. 'That's a good idea. Barbara will know. . .'

Ellie followed Dr Carmody into the quarters, trying not to smile at the man who had more the air of an absent-minded professor than a doctor in charge of a hospital.

'Sister Standish — welcome aboard.' Dr Simon Taverner put out his hand, and Ellie shook it. 'That's the last time I'll call you that, of course,' he added. 'You're in the country now. We don't use formality. I'm Simon.'

Ellie had already discovered it was true. Sister Barbara Knox had called all the doctors, even the super, by their first names as she had shown Ellie her room and provided a guided tour of the quarters. Barbara was the sister in charge of the surgical ward, and a native of Berringar. She was a friendly, freckled countrywoman, about five years older than Ellie, and Ellie had liked her immediately.

'We've got the top floor, and the men — the doctors — have the bottom. The dining-room and common-room are on the bottom in the eastern wing. Nice there. The sun comes in at breakfast.'

'Do we have the same dining-room?' Ellie had asked shyly.

'Yes, it's all in together here. This is the country.'

Simon Taverner had echoed her words when Ellie had found him in the common-room after finishing her unpacking. 'Make yourself at home,' he added now. 'I'm going to light this fire. It's cool for April.'

The old hospital building was made of local sand-stone, Australian style, with high ceilings and wide verandas. The room they were in, the common-room, was a cosy place with a huge open fire and comfortable if rather battered armchairs. The dining-room opened out of it, with solid old-fashioned furniture and a servery down one side.

Simon plied her with questions as he bent to light the fire. Where did she live in Sydney? What did she do with her spare time? And then, with a quizzical look, had she left a boyfriend behind?

Ellie found herself blushing a little.

'You might as well answer,' he said cheerfully. 'This is a small town. We'll find out everything about you eventually.' Ellie laughed, and Simon continued, 'For example, I already know that you fed the kangaroos with Charlie Carmody this afternoon. You can't hide anything here.'

'Apparently not,' she smiled.

Simon darted her a conspiratorial look that made his glinting eyes brim with mischief. He lowered his voice. 'We don't *think* Charlie's mad, but he's not like the rest of us.'

Ellie couldn't help a little choke of laughter, but she said quickly, 'I thought he seemed very kind.'

'Oh, yes,' Simon said carelessly. 'He's harmless.'

And once again Ellie caught that note of arrogance — or patronage — she had heard at her interview. Simon Taverner was handsome and she was sure he could be charming, but she was not too sure she was going to like him.

There were ten of them at dinner. Matron was married, Ellie learned, and had her own cottage. Many of the hospital personnel lived in town. But three other single sisters, Barbara among them, lived in quarters. Besides the three senior doctors, all of them bachelors, there were also three young house surgeons who spent six months here as part of their training at Canberra Hospital.

They sat at two tables, and after the rigid protocol of Royal North Shore it was strange to find that there was no distinction made between doctors and nurses, and that surnames were never heard.

Pete, Colin, James, Mary, Alison. Ellie memorised the names that went with the faces. In time she might know them as well as her own family. Feeling very much the new girl, unused to mixing with medical staff on terms of equality, Ellie answered the polite enquiries of her new comrades, but mostly tried to listen and store away information.

'Charlie — did you remember to look at Mr Hill?' Paul Vassy suddenly bethought himself of a medical problem.

Charlie Carmody looked up from his plate and nodded.

'Thank God for that,' Paul said, as though it had been by no means a certain thing. 'Well, so, can you give this man an anaesthetic?'

Ellie realised with something of a shock that Charlie Carmody, in additon to being the medical superintendent, was also the hospital's anaesthetist.

Charlie nodded placidly, continuing to eat his dinner.

'Who? Not old Ernie Hill?' asked Mary, the medical sister. 'Lord, with a heart and lungs like his, I wouldn't have thought he'd survive it. What's wrong with him now?'

'Carcinoma of the bowel,' answered Paul. 'Not very big. If I can operate, I can remove it. There are better ways to die than cancer of the bowel.'

'General anaesthesia, for example,' Simon put in smoothly.

Paul glanced at him. 'If Charlie says he can do it, he can,' he said flatly.

Simon held up his hands. 'Just a joke,' he declared.

But Ellie had already found herself wondering what sort of anaesthetist Dr Carmody would make. Anaesthetics as a career was said to consist of nine parts boredom and one part terror. She knew that no speciality required more presence of mind or swifter judgement. Most people thought of the anaesthetist as someone who put them to sleep. But he had a much more important job than that—that of making sure they woke up again. Without the anaesthetist's consent, no operation could go forward. It was he who decided whether a patient could withstand the procedure, and he who would, if necessary, call it off in the middle. He must take into account every detail of the patient's medical history in order to pilot him safely through it. And if the patient died on the table, it was his responsibility.

If the patient were sick enough, the anaesthetist would look after him in Intensive Care till he once again had a firm enough grip on life to be handed back to the surgeon.

The days of ether were long gone. Now it was a complex, critical, highly technical speciality calling for compendious knowledge and swift, certain judgement.

Ellie glanced at Dr Carmody and tried to imagine it. He seemed to do everything with slow deliberation, and to be lost at least half the time in reverie. In the contemplation of it, Ellie's imagination failed her.

The incident in the common-room later didn't imbue her with any more confidence. They had retired there after dinner, Charlie Carmody to an armchair on one side of the fire, where he read for a while before dropping his journal down on the hearth, perhaps to listen to the others or perhaps to indulge in another fit of abstraction.

Ellie was discovering that several of her colleagues were keen outdoorsmen like herself.

'We should take you up to meet the park rangers,' Simon was saying. 'Two fellows and a girl. Always climbing cliffs and abseiling into canyons.' He gave his white smile. 'I'll happily watch you from the bottom, or the top, as the case may be.'

'They are nice people,' Paul put in. 'They are good friends of Charlie.'

Barbara Knox sniffed the air, and cut across their conversation. 'What's that smell?' she demanded. 'Something's burning.'

'The fire?' murmured Simon.

But Paul Vassy had seen the smoke and leapt to his feet. 'Charlie! But you are an idiot! Do you see and smell nothing?' He darted in beside Charlie's chair, and began to stamp on a smouldering edition of the *British Medical Journal*. 'Why do you put it so close to the fire?' Paul demanded, holding up the charred relic.

Charlie Carmody ran his hand through his hair in what Ellie guessed was a gesture of embarrassment. His face held a remorseful look that made her want to laugh. 'That's a pity,' he remarked. 'There was something I wanted to read in that.'

'A really hot article,' Simon suggested, and they all laughed out loud, Charlie Carmody included.

Ellie couldn't help but return the grin Simon Taverner gave her. 'You haven't seen anything yet,' he said in a low voice.

CHAPTER TWO

'IT's a really well-equipped casualty,' Ellie said in some surprise.

Simon Taverner, perched on the side of her desk at one end of the casualty area, nodded his sleek head. 'It has to be. We're a long way from a major hospital, even by air. We've got to be able to handle everything here.'

'Well, we have the stuff to do it with,' she acknowledged.

'I suppose you find it strange not to have a casualty specialist with you. But anything Pete Russell can't handle one of us will come and deal with. You may find Charlie and Paul in Theatre sometimes, but I — ' he flashed his gleaming smile ' — I am always at your service.'

Ellie felt much more at home after only four days. She was pleased with her little kingdom on the ground floor of the new three-storey hospital building. The house surgeon who worked there was inexperienced — in his first year — but he was eager to learn and easy to get along with. She had worried about the nurses who would be under her, wondering if they would feel she was too young for the position, but they seemed to accept her without resentment. Even Caroline, who was much older than she and with more nursing years behind her, seemed to find it natural that someone with a casualty certificate from North Shore should be in charge and did not envy her.

'Are you finding it busy enough?' Simon asked. 'Or do you pine for the wail of sirens at North Shore?'

'Not one bit,' Ellie answered. 'I like having enough time to do the job well. And it's busier than I thought a country cas would be. People come from much further away than I expected. They seem to come from places with their own hospitals.'

'They do,' Simon agreed. 'The Base has the reputation of being the best.' He grinned. 'Such wonderful doctors and nurses, you know.'

'Well, that must make you proud,' she said.

Simon placed his hand over his heart. 'It gives me a warm feeling.'

Ellie couldn't help giggling. She was finding Simon more likeable than she had expected. He had a sardonic air and a satirical sense of humour, but he was prepared to put himself out to be helpful. Ellie was surprised at how much she saw of him, and of Charlie Carmody too, who seemed to wander into Cas whenever he had nothing else to do, sometimes to help and guide Pete Russell, and sometimes to do nothing more than sit at her desk and get in her way.

That wasn't hard for him. He took up a lot of space. Pete said he was six feet four and, with a large frame to match, he was a great hulk of a man. It was lucky he had such a placid disposition. Ellie thought her first impression had been right—Charlie was a quiet man with a habit of vagueness and sometimes a clumsiness that could exasperate his colleagues, but he was also beloved for his great good nature.

'Charlie's great!' Pete had said, and Ellie knew he wasn't the only one to think so.

'What's that chap's problem?' asked Simon as the porter wheeled an elderly man back into Casualty.

'Pete thinks he has a kidney stone. He's had an

X-ray. Pete's going to look at it when he gets back from lunch.'

'He doesn't look as though he's enjoying himself,' Simon observed. 'Has he had some morphine?'

Ellie nodded, and told him how much.

'Yes, that's typical,' Simon commented, his air a little patronising. 'They never give enough morphine, these boys.'

'He's a fairly old man,' Ellie offered.

Simon smiled. 'Tough as old boots. You couldn't kill him with twice as much. Do you want me to look at the X-ray?'

'That'd be kind,' said Ellie.

'Anything for you, Sister,' he said in a bantering tone. 'Any time.'

Ellie placed the X-ray on the lighted screen. She was experienced enough not to need Simon to point out the stone in the ureter, halfway between Herb Wright's right kidney and his bladder. But he did so anyway, and told her that it was probably a calcium stone. Herb would be found to have too much calcium in his blood, and to spend a lot of his time dehydrated, from working on his farm in the sum.

'Painful business,' Simon commented. 'Worse than childbirth, they say. The pain comes from the ureter, which goes into spasm trying to pass it. Looks like a job for Paul to get that out. Too big to pass.'

'I've seen ones that size pass,' Ellie said timidly. 'I thought maybe we could try. If I give him heaps of water to drink and a hot shower. . .'

Simon gave a sardonic smile. 'Is that the nursing solution? Well, by all means try. But I don't think you'll succeed.' His tone was just a little condescending.

Ellie ignored it. Many doctors disliked the nursing

staff making suggestions. 'The trouble is I don't have a strainer to strain his urine.'

'Sister Standish, to demonstrate my goodwill I'll even get you a strainer.'

And when Simon returned with one, purloined from the kitchens, ten minutes later Ellie thought one really had to forgive a little condescension in the face of such helpfulness.

'I'll do anything not to have an operation,' declared Herb Wright when Ellie suggested it. 'I'll stand on me blinking head.' And, true to his word, he manfully swallowed the fluids that Ellie plied him with over the next few hours till he said he had to go or bust. At that point, Ellie led him to the shower.

'It seems to help you relax,' she explained. 'I can't really give you a scientific explanation.'

'Wouldn't understand it if you did,' said Herb, obediently taking the strainer.

'Just shout if you need help,' Ellie advised. But she wasn't about to go far away, with an old man who'd had a shot of morphine under the shower.

'Doesn't look like he's going to pass out, does he?' asked Pete, pausing between patients.

'No. He looks all right,' Ellie reassured him.

Even so, she moved like lightning when she did hear Herb shout. 'What is it, Herb? are you all right?'

But the grizzled head sticking out from behind the shower curtain was wearing a grin. 'You little beauty!' he said, and held up between a thumb and forefinger a roughly round object the size of a five-cent piece.

Herb Wright bestowed the prize on Ellie. Simon, later congratulating her with a good grace, said it should be strung on a chain for Ellie to wear round her neck.

* * *

'She might make you redundant, Paul,' Simon joked, when Ellie's cure was announced at dinnertime.

Ellie found herself blushing, all the more when Simon came to stand beside her and placed an arm round her shoulders.

'We've definitely chosen the right person for the job,' he declared. 'A colleague to be proud of.' But there was nothing very colleague-like about the way he stroked her upper arm with his hand, or indeed in the glinting blue eyes that looked down at her. Ellie wondered whether Simon flirted with all the nursing staff, or whether he could really be interested in her. She thought she saw a small sardonic smile on Paul's face, but Charlie Carmody looked on as placidly as ever.

It was Barbara Knox who brought up the subject after dinner, when she passed the open door of Ellie's room. 'Hey, that looks home-like!' she said, and Ellie invited her in.

Ellie was pleased with her room. It was quite large, and looked out towards the ranges. There was a comfortable bed which now bore her quilt, two armchairs, a set of bookshelves, quite a good desk, a wardrobe and a chest of drawers. A cupboard with a sink completed the furnishings and allowed her to make tea in her room. When she had put her things away, arranged her books on the shelves, hung her pictures and thrown the woven rug on the floor, it was quite a cosy little home.

'Feel like a cup of tea?' Ellie asked, and Barbara lost no time in settling into the other chair.

'I think Simon likes you,' was her forthright comment a little later. 'I hear he's taken to haunting Cas.'

'Doesn't he usually?' Ellie asked hesitantly.

Barbara grinned. 'Not him. Charlie's always there.

He likes to help the houseman. Not Simon. You got a boyfriend?' she asked abruptly.

'No — not at the moment,' Ellie admitted.

'Well, you won't have to look far,' Barbara gave her opinion.

'Hasn't Simon a girlfriend?' asked Ellie curiously.

'He *was* seeing one of the nurses from Bega Hospital. Looks to me like he's decided why drive all the way to Bega when you can get what you want at home.'

Ellie laughed, but she wondered with a little indignation whether it was confidently assumed that Simon could get whatever he wanted. 'Well, I hardly know him at the moment,' she observed calmly, thinking that Barbara was probably wrong anyway. 'And I didn't come here looking for romance.'

Barbara gave her cheerful grin. 'Oh, it's got a way of finding you,' she said.

Bessie Lucknow was not having a good day. The ambulance brought the old lady in during the morning with an oxygen mask on her face, but she was still gasping for breath and looking a little blue.

'Heart condition,' said the ambulance officer helpfully. 'Been here lots of times.'

Pete Russell took one look at her and said, 'Better get Simon,' but Ellie had seen plenty of patients in heart failure and knew what she ought to do while they waited for Simon to appear.

'Help me do an ECG, please, Caroline, while we're waiting,' she said quietly, and Pete said,

'That's a good idea. Why didn't I think of that?' in his endearingly honest way.

'Nursing job,' said Ellie, to save his face a little. 'Do you want me to get a mobile chest X-ray done?'

'That's another good idea,' said Pete, and Ellie had

to stop herself from grinning. It was really hard being
a brand-new doctor. Ellie had dealt with this problem
many more times than he had.

It wasn't long before Simon was there, and with the
chest X-ray the diagnosis was easy to make — pulmo-
nary oedema. Bessie's heart wasn't pumping properly
and fluid had built up in her lungs till she couldn't
breathe. One day it would probably kill her, but not
today. Ellie had the drugs ready even before Simon
asked for them. She knew what he'd give her through
the cannula he'd placed in the vein of her hand. Lasix
and morphine and perhaps some others, and anginine
tablets placed under her tongue.

In an hour Bessie was looking much better, and
could breathe well enough to answer Simon's questions
more fully than she had before. Yes, she had had
angina the last few days. She'd been spring-cleaning.
She had people coming to stay. Yes, she had been
ignoring it a bit. She had to get the work done.

Simon shook his head. 'You've been a very naughty
girl.' It was kindly said, but even so Ellie didn't like it.
It was patronising to speak to an elderly woman like
that. But so many doctors did.

Bessie Lucknow looked embarrassed. 'Yeah, well, I
s'pose I should've taken a bit more notice.'

'You certainly should've. Never mind, sweetie. We'll
put you in hospital for a few days. If you're a good girl,
we'll let you go home early next week.' Ellie didn't like
the 'sweetie' any more than the rest. She was pleased
to see that Pete didn't copy it when he took Bessie's
history for the admission notes.

Ellie prepared the nursing admission notes, phoned
Bessie's family to let them know what was happening,
and stationed the next patient in one of the cubicles for

Pete to see, by which time Charlie Carmody had strolled into Cas.

Bessie seemed to know him well. 'Hello, Dr Carmody!' she called. She sounded pleased to see him.

Charlie came to stand, grinning, at the end of her bed. 'Hello, Mrs Lucknow,' he said formally.

'Oh, all right!' she said, laughing. 'Hello, Charlie.'

'Hello, Bessie,' he answered sweetly.

It surprised a ripple of laughter from Ellie. Bessie Lucknow turned to her. 'He's a wicked one for pulling your leg, this one,' she said with high enjoyment.

Ellie was surprised. She would never have thought it.

'What are you doing here, Bessie?' he asked.

'Oh, this stupid ticker of mine. I guess I've been doing too much.'

'You must have considered it worth it,' he said with deliberation.

'It wasn't worth it!' she said emphatically. 'In future, my guests can come to a dirty house.'

Charlie gave his slow grin and enveloped her hand in his big paw. 'Hand 'em a broom at the door,' he said blithely.

Everything was ready for Bessie Lucknow to be wheeled upstairs to the medical ward in a remarkably short time.

'Thanks, love,' the old lady called to Ellie as she was leaving. 'You were beaut!' Ellie returned her cheery wave and smile, and thought, What a nice old lady. Patients often forgot to thank the nursing staff, and sometimes they did more for them than the doctors.

Ellie turned back to the work of Casualty with satisfaction. At the end of her first week, she was beginning to feel she had things under control. It was an assessment with which her colleagues agreed as they snatched a cup of tea together at the end of the shift.

'She's great,' said Caroline Tuckey. 'She really knows her stuff. And she's organised.'

'Yes. She's really calm, too. Nothing throws her,' agreed Chris, the next most experienced nurse.

Vanessa Peach, who had only just graduated, also had her opinion. 'She's nice, isn't she? She doesn't make you feel like an idiot when you don't know something. And she always seems to know when you need help.'

Peter Russell had also lounged in for a quick cuppa. 'The patients like her,' he observed. 'She's got a great sense of humour. She makes them feel like she cares about them.'

'She's pretty, too,' said Vanessa, adding plaintively, 'It's not fair.'

Ellie would have been not a little embarrassed to have heard their conversation, but she was handing over to the evening sister in Casualty, and when she had completed that task there was Simon Taverner, parked once again on a corner of her desk.

'I'll walk you to quarters,' he offered. 'Had a good day?'

'Yes. No major catastrophes.' She gave her grin as she collected her bag.

'Well, you've got to the end of your first week,' he said as they left the hospital building. 'I think that calls for a celebration. There are three passable places to eat in Berringar. Like most country towns — the Chinese, the Italian and the pub. Take your pick.'

Ellie gave a shy little chuckle. 'That's very kind of you,' she said.

'Not at all. If I don't eat something besides hospital food one night a week, my taste-buds'll hold a stop work meeting.'

'I think mine have staged a walk-out,' said Ellie.

'North Shore has the worst food on the planet, and I've been eating it for years. And the worrying thing is I was getting to like it.'

Simon gave a rich laugh. 'We'll definitely have to do something about that. You'll be doing me a favour if you come with me.'

'Thank you,' she said. 'I'd like to eat out. I'd like to get to know the town — and I'll drive us there, too, so I can get used to getting about around here. But it has to be Dutch.' Ellie liked Simon more than she had expected, but she didn't want him to get the idea that she was looking for more than a friend.

He looked down at her with a sardonic glint of amusement. 'If that'll make you feel more comfortable,' he said, and immediately made her feel *less* comfortable.

The feeling of awkwardness left, however, soon after they sat down in the dining-room of the Town and Country hotel. Simon Taverner knew just how to put a woman at her ease, Ellie realised. He was an interesting companion — clever, entertaining and witty. He had an observant eye for the foibles of his fellows and could be wickedly and amusingly satirical. If he also sounded at times a little cruel, and if his charm seemed a little practised, Ellie didn't care. She had come to the end of a hard week, and was prepared to enjoy herself.

That willingness didn't extend, however, to letting him kiss her when they finally climbed back into the car to return to the hospital. Ellie pulled back as Simon smiled at her, then slid his hand behind her neck and leaned towards her.

Immediately he withdrew. 'How gauche of me!' he remarked at once, and sat looking at her, his eyes reflecting the glow of a street-lamp. 'What can I say, my Ellie? I can only plead the effect of wine and those uniquely green eyes of yours. . .'

Ellie could well believe in the effect of the wine. She had been surprised at how much he'd drunk.

'Have I sunk myself beneath reproach? Will you refuse ever to relieve the tedium of my life and eat with me again?' His tone was one of mock-entreaty.

'Of course not,' Ellie said, determined not to make a big deal of it. 'But I only want to be friends right now, Simon.'

Abruptly he held out his hand. 'Friends right now,' he avowed, and Ellie saw him grin as she shook it.

When she parked the car in her spot at the back of the quarters, Ellie was surprised to see the large bulk of Charlie Carmody looming out of the semi-darkness.

'What's he doing out here at eleven o'clock?' she asked curiously.

Simon gave her another grin. 'Ah!' he said mysteriously. 'Another of our leader's little eccentricities. Come on. I'll show you.'

Charlie seemed to be crouching in front of an enclosure that Ellie had earlier taken to be a country hospital's fowl run, but he had heard Simon's car, and greeted them quietly as they approached.

'Ellie wants to know what you're doing,' Simon said, and Charlie looked up with his shy smile.

'Just feeding the possums. I'm a little late.'

'Do you keep possums in a fowl run?' Ellie asked wonderingly.

'Well, these fellows,' he explained, 'they're special. They're pigmy possums and they're dying out. I'm trying to breed them. It's an interest of mine,' he added rather apologetically.

'Oh! Can we see them?' asked Ellie, interested.

'Yes. They're too busy eating to care,' he said, and switched on his torch.

Ellie gave little cry of delight as the torch beam picked out a furry animal the size of a small cat. His coat was soft grey with darker stripes, and he waved a bushy dark grey tail as he ate. He did look up for a moment as if to enquire into the necessity for the light, and Ellie saw a dear little face peering up—a furry little face with a pink button nose, delicate whiskers, soft grey ears and big, dark, gentle eyes.

'He's beautiful!' she breathed, and in the torchlight saw Charlie smile.

'Yes. There are three. He's a young male. There's an older male and a female.'

'You do have a grip on the basics, then, Charlie,' Simon quipped.

Charlie Carmody bore the raillery with his usual cheerful good nature. He flashed the torch round. 'You can't see the female. She's in those bushes.' He moved the light again and revealed a large male who gave an affronted glare.

'He's much bigger than the other one,' Ellie observed. 'He looks rather battle-scarred. One of his ears is hanging down, and there's a piece out of it.'

'Yes, he's much older, that one. He's seen a few battles.'

'Will he be too old to breed?' Ellie asked.

Charlie's deep, quiet voice was decided. 'Oh, no. He's got it in him yet. He's very strong. He's a survivor—a good fighter. Good genes to pass.' He turned to her with a smile lurking in his eyes. 'I've got my money on him.'

Ellie smiled back. 'Are they a threatened species?' she asked, and he nodded.

'Not enough of them to find breeding partners. The

rangers found these ones and brought them here. They know it's an interest of mine. I've bred some other animals for them.'

'I think it's a wonderful thing to do!' said Ellie warmly.

'You don't think that one's a little limp-wristed?' asked Simon mischievously, and Ellie giggled.

Charlie grinned and stuck some more feed through the wire. 'Don't listen to him, Hercules,' he murmured kindly.

Simon gave a staccato laugh. 'Hercules! You call that poor little animal Hercules?' Ellie couldn't help laughing too.

It worried Charlie not at all. He continued to give his cheerful grin, and merely said, 'I liked it,' in a contented tone.

'I like it too,' Ellie said with her elfin smile, and was rewarded with another of his own.

'Well, I'm getting bitten by things out here,' Simon complained. 'I suggest we leave Dr Doolittle to it. It looks like gluttony rather than lust is the order of the day today.'

CHAPTER THREE

'*PARBLEU*! I cannot find this man's old notes!' said Paul in exasperation. 'Charlie has taken them to do a discharge summary. His office is like the sty of ten pigs!'

'I'll have a look, Dr Vassy,' offered Vanessa. 'I've found things in there before. I seem to know how Dr Carmody's mind works.'

'That is a worry,' Paul said wryly as she went away, and made Ellie chuckle.

In the space of a few weeks Ellie felt she had really begun to know her new colleagues, and even to be able to call some of them friends. She had become familiar with Caroline Tuckey's placid nature and dry sense of humour, with Chris Bates' direct speech and young Vanessa's cheerful muddle-headedness. Ellie worked days, as there was a permanent evening sister, and each day one of them worked with her, according to their roster. She liked them all, but it was Caroline, with her broad experience and calm humour, whom it was most rewarding to work with. Ellie had wondered why Caroline hadn't applied for the job she held, and had said so.

Caroline had shaken her light curls. 'No. Not me. I like to be one of the team. Less worry. I like to feel relaxed.'

It *was* a responsibility, running the department, but it was one which Ellie, with her quick intelligence and energetic efficiency, thrived on. It wasn't long before the doctors realised that they could rely on her to have everything at her fingertips.

'You know this patient requires a Steinmann pin, Ellie?' asked Paul Vassy.

Ellie nodded and led him to the X-ray screen where the films showing the man's fractured femur were already mounted. Paul Vassy examined them and grunted. '*Alors*, we begin. You know what I require?'

'All ready,' Ellie said, preceding him to the patient's bedside where all the equipment was neatly set out.

Paul Vassy ran his eye over it. 'Of course,' he murmured. 'I make my apologies for being so stupid.'

Ellie liked Paul Vassy very much. He was outspoken and irascible. He managed it without offending, perhaps because he was impartial with his insults, bestowing them at times on everyone, including himself. Or perhaps it was because he was also quick to praise. Criticism or praise, his opinion was well worth having. His mind darted ahead with the same sort of quickness one saw in the movements of his gesticulating hands and his piercing dark eyes.

Ellie stood by to help as Paul, with Pete Russell's aid, performed the barbaric-looking procedure of drilling a hole through the top of the patient's tibia with what looked for all the world like a carpenter's hand drill. A steel pin would then be slid into the hole and used to provide traction to keep the broken femur in the right position for healing. As always, Paul's movements were quick and sure.

Vanessa, having returned triumphant, paused for a moment near Ellie to look, and uttered involuntarily, 'Yuk!' as the drill ground its way noisily through bone. Ellie heard her swallow, and glanced up from where she was helping to immobilise the leg of the anaesthetised patient. The young nurse's face had paled.

'If you're going to faint, Vanessa, go and do it on that empty bed over there,' she recommended, adding cheerfully, 'And try to vomit on the floor, not the bed. Then you won't have to change it.'

Paul Vassy gave a crack of laughter. 'Our so practical Ellie! What did we do without you?'

On Ellie's days off, she had explored the town. She had also had dinner twice more with Simon, and one Sunday had lunch with him at the fine old colonial pub in company with some of the staff from the medical wards. Simon was at his best in a crowd. He had the wit and spirit to be the life of the party. And it was flattering to be marked out by him for special attention. It was also a shade embarrassing. Ellie could see that some of the staff were beginning to assume there was a romance between them.

'I hear you're the outdoor type, Ellie,' remarked one of the nurses from Medical. 'Are we going to see you take to the Great Outdoors, Simon?' From the laughter it provoked, Ellie guessed that it was not Simon's usual form of recreation.

He gave his even white grin. 'I've got the bush-walking boots on order, Sue.'

Ellie blushed a little as he turned to her, blue eyes twinkling with laughter, and she found herself wondering as she surveyed the smoothly handsome features whether she *would* welcome a romance with Simon. There were any number of others who would, she knew. His interest was definitely very flattering.

'To prove myself, I'll take you to meet the park rangers next weekend,' he promised.

Ellie had been wanting to visit the park, and was glad to think there were some people there who might share her interests. She had to admit to herself that she was not averse to the thought of doing it in the company of Simon. 'I'd like that,' she said, and two housemen who had been admiring her mentally wrote her down as taken. Simon Taverner was stiff opposition.

On the way back to the Base in Simon's car, Ellie asked, 'Do you mean it about next Sunday?'

'Of course,' Simon answered.

Ellie tried to find the right words to say to him. 'The only thing is, Simon, if we spend too much time together people will think we're an item.'

Simon slid into his parking space and turned off the engine. 'That would be a shame,' he said with a mocking grin.

'Well, it wouldn't be right,' she returned.

Simon turned towards her, still smiling. 'It could be right,' he said softly, and when Ellie didn't answer added, 'You know — you could just try kissing me once. You never know, you *might* like it.' His tone was teasing, but Ellie thought he had no doubt that she *would* like it.

'I'm sure others have,' she said as lightly as she could.

Simon's rather dainty mouth curved into a smile that Ellie thought was a little self-satisfied. 'Is *that* what's worrying you?' he said loftily.

'No!' Ellie hastened to erase the idea he'd taken. 'I couldn't care less about anyone else. It's just that I hardly know you.'

'It's hard to see how you're going to know me, if you keep holding me at arm's length,' he said in a tone of amusement. And before she knew what he was about he had seized her head with hands that were surprisingly strong and brought his lips to hers in a kiss that was meant to tantalise. He let her go in an instant, and sat laughing down at her. 'That wasn't so terrible, was it?' he asked with what Ellie thought was a disagreeable hint of smugness.

Ellie was annoyed. It hadn't been terrible, but she hadn't wanted it; and she was almost certain that Charlie Carmody, crossing the lawn to the possums' house, had seen it. 'If you do that again, I won't go anywhere with you,' she promised.

Simon gave a careless laugh. 'Have I disturbed your equanimity?' he asked in a provocative tone.

Ellie could see that it would never occur to Simon that a woman might not want his overtures. He was abominably conceited.

Suddenly he gave a rueful smile. 'Oh, dear. You do look angry. And I like you so much, Ellie. What can I do to make amends?' The sincerely contrite tone was disarming.

It suddenly occurred to Ellie that women had probably never given Simon any reason to doubt his attractions. It was hard not to be a little conceited when they fell at your feet.

'Just be friendly, Simon,' she said firmly.

'You think that was a little over-friendly?' he asked wistfully, and she couldn't help laughing.

'Yes!'

'Oh, well. I'll do better in future,' he vowed. 'Only — you are so very beautiful, Ellie. It's hard not to have some lapses.'

Ellie would not have been human had she not felt a little glow of pleasure at that.

Charlie had the kettle on, Ellie was pleased to see, when she came down to the dining-room after changing from the clothes she had worn out to lunch into jeans and sweater. There were several hours till dinner and she felt like a cup of tea.

She also felt a little awkward, knowing that Charlie had witnessed that kiss of Simon's. But Charlie seemed as vaguely amiable as ever, and he merely glanced up from his medical journal to give her a genial smile when she put a tea-bag into a cup for herself.

'How's Hercules?' she asked, schooling herself to be normal, and his smile broadened and lit his grey eyes. Charlie had a nice face, she decided.

'He's biding his time,' he said.

'Won't the young one mate with her first?' asked Ellie.

'He might,' he said. 'He's attempting to interest her. Going through the ritual of courtship.'

'What's Hercules doing meanwhile?'

Charlie's mouth curved up again. 'Looking on in bored contempt,' he said.

Ellie gave a peal of laughter, then, 'Do you think he remembers the ritual?' she asked.

There was a little pause, during which Charlie continued to smile, then he answered softly, 'Oh, yes. He remembers.'

'Ellie!' Barbara's face appeared in the doorway. 'Do you know there are letters in your pigeon-hole?'

Ellie hadn't checked for a few days. The kettle wasn't quite boiling yet, so she went out into the vestibule to see. There was a letter from her mother, and a few less interesting window-faces. She sat on the stairs, and read the former with her usual pleasure. Her mother wrote the same kind of letter Ellie did—vivid and funny. At length she finished and folded it up again to put in her pocket. Paul Vassy came in as she returned to the dining-room, where Charlie was once again absorbed in his journal.

'Hasn't that jug boiled yet?' she asked. It wasn't the sort that switched itself off.

'Oh, no!' Paul Vassy ejaculated. 'There is steam all over the wall! Charlie, you imbecile! You have done it again!' He snatched up the silent kettle to look inside, and said, 'But yes! Again!' at which point Charlie finally looked up from his journal.

His eyes travelled from Paul Vassy's face to the kettle Paul brandished, and he uttered a groan. Ellie clapped her hand over her mouth in order not to laugh at the ludicrously rueful expression on his face. He *was* the med super. It was all right for Paul to call him an imbecile, but Ellie didn't feel she ought to laugh.

'How many?' Paul demanded. 'How many now? I will tell you, Charlie! Four!' He turned to Ellie and made a Gallic gesture of despair.

Slowly Ellie brought herself under control and removed her hand from her mouth. 'I'll go and boil a saucepan, shall I?' she said in only a slightly shaking voice.

Paul seemed to have resigned himself to Charlie's latest misdemeanour by dinnertime, enough at least to discuss tomorrow's surgery with him. 'That is going to be a long operation, that gastrectomy,' he observed. 'You are happy with him, Charlie?'

Charlie nodded slowly. 'We'll have to be careful,' he observed. 'And he'll have to go to ICU afterwards.' They had a small ward with four beds that doubled as Intensive Care and Coronary Care. The patients there were Charlie's responsibility.

Once again, Ellie found herself wondering how a man of Charlie Carmody's absence of mind could possibly manage that sort of task. Evidently, he did. The man with the bad lungs and heart had survived his bowel resection and done very well. For the first time,

Ellie really studied Charlie Carmody's face. He had a strong face, she thought — very different from Simon's smoothly good-looking one. His jaw was square, and looked determined. His mouth, larger than Simon's dainty one, was set in a reposeful curve that bespoke his good humour. The eyes she had noticed before were a clear grey, with little smile lines at the corner. The brows and hair were dark brown, the forehead high. It was quite a distinguished face when you thought about it — intelligent and manly. But he was such a klutz. She still couldn't imagine him in Intensive Care. The man was an enigma.

It was Simon who drew attention to Charlie's latest lapse after dinner. 'Where's the kettle?' he said.

Paul Vassy made a richly expressive gesture towards his superior.

'I see,' said Simon drily. 'We really will have to get one that switches off, won't we? Or ban Charlie from using it. That may be the better course. Something tells me that, however sophisticated the apparatus, our beloved leader will find some way of disabling it.'

It was funny. Ellie couldn't help laughing a little with the others. But she also felt sorry for Charlie. It couldn't be nice to have people poking fun at you all the time. She was only amazed that he took it so philosophically. Even so, she wasn't sure that there wasn't a little tinge of red in his face this time, and she was sorry when Simon continued to rib him long past what seemed kind.

'I've contacted the ranger station, and they'll be pleased if we visit on Sunday,' Simon told her in Casualty next day.

'Oh, good,' said Ellie. 'Will I take my boots? I mean, you probably don't want to go walking, do you?'

'Certainly. Anything you want to do,' he said.

'What about something to eat?' asked Ellie.

'Leave that to me,' he said.

'Oh, no, but——' Ellie began, but he interrupted her.

'You're working this Saturday. I'll have much more time.' He smiled. 'Don't worry. I'm surprisingly good at throwing together a picnic.'

'That's kind,' said Ellie.

'I was hoping you'd think so,' he joked.

'Can you get me some 4–0 silk, please, Chris?' Ellie heard Peter Russell say, and she glanced over to see that Chris had everything ready for Pete to sew up a young footballer's forehead.

Simon looked too and, frowning, got up to go and stand beside him. 'You're not going to use silk on that cut, are you?' he asked abruptly.

Pete looked back questioningly.

Simon made a noise of impatience. 'Don't they teach you boys anything before they send you out here?' he demanded.

Peter flushed to the roots of his hair.

'Never use a silk suture on a face. Use nylon. Silk leaves more of a scar. Surely someone must have told you that?' Simon's tone was insulting.

Sympathy for Pete welled up in Ellie. Really, there was no need for Simon to take that tone, especially in front of the patient. And it was a pretty academic point in this case, anyway. The young footie player on the bed didn't look as though he could care less what kind of scar he had on a face that already bore plenty of others. Most of them had probably not seen the attention of a doctor at all. Ellie was annoyed with Simon. How could he be so nice one moment, and so — well, yes — nasty the next?

Ellie accompanied him to the door of Cas when he left, determined to put in a good word for Pete. 'He's a good house officer, you know,' she said gently.

There was a pause, then Simon said, 'Oh, did you think I was too harsh?' There was an unpleasant sort of irony in his voice as he added, 'But you have a soft heart. You'll have to allow me to be the judge, I think.' He glanced in Pete's direction and said in a tone of fine arrogance that Ellie was sure was audible, 'I find him amazingly ignorant, actually.'

Ellie shook her head as the cas door closed behind Simon. Every now and then she wondered whether she did like him after all. But her sense of justice asserted itself. It must be hard, when you were so knowledge-able and experienced yourself, to be continually watch-ing beginners make mistakes; and hard also, when you held people's lives in your hands, not to be just a trifle arrogant. But she wished all the same he could have handled it differently. When Charlie corrected Pete, he was almost apologetic. Oh, well. That was Charlie. And as Edna, the cleaning lady, said, Charlie was an original.

However, Ellie couldn't complain about Simon's behaviour as he drove her up into Goolcoola National Park on Sunday. He was in high spirits, and never more charming or entertaining. The park was an area of wild and breathtaking beauty—of dense eucalypt forest, sheer escarpments and spectacular river chasms. Ellie was spellbound as they climbed up the mountain-side on to the plateau, and finally in through the park gates. There was a pine-log office there, but Simon kept driving.

'They'll be at the quarters,' he said. 'Tony said they'd be working on their truck till we came.'

* * *

'Brown! Five-eighth! That's not five-eighth!' The voice which came from under the Land Cruiser was exasperated, its statements punctuated by the hurling of a spanner at the dark girl in park ranger's uniform who crouched beside the car with the tools spread out before her.

'W-wasn't it?' she stammered. 'I'm sorry. I thought it was.' She rifled in the tool-box for another spanner, peering in a myopic way at the numbers stamped on the handles, as there came from under the car a sigh and the words,

'Don't think, Brown.'

Simon grinned down at Ellie before making their presence known.

'Oh, hi!' the girl cried, spinning round. 'I thought I heard a car, but Tony said it was in my head!'

Ellie was introduced to Marian Brown, and liked what she saw. Dark-haired, with a rounded open face that Ellie thought very pretty, Marian was softly spoken and rather shy. Despite this, Ellie thought she would be easy to get to know, for she was utterly straightforward. There was no sham or pretence about Marian Brown. Ellie thought she would turn out to be what she looked — a kind, friendly and generally cheerful girl who could be relied upon.

Something like a muttered imprecation issued from under the Land Cruiser. Marian peered under it. 'What did you say, Tony?' she asked faithfully.

'I said give me the pipe wrench, woman. You going deaf?' was the rude reply.

'Yeah, you give it to him, precious,' said a newcomer. 'Someplace soft.'

Ellie giggled and shook hands with the slight, sandy-haired man who had emerged from the quarters building. His name was John, but he was always called JB.

Sliding out from under the car some time later, Tony Gallagher shook hands with Simon and said 'Good day' to Ellie. He then turned to rap, 'Brown! You going to get me a rag?' and Ellie's eyebrows rose as Marian scuttled off, to reappear with an old shirt, on which he began to wipe the grease off his hands and forearms. He was a good-looking man, in rather a fierce, untidy way. He was tall, with dark hair that curled and light hazel eyes, and his character had all the force and dominance that Ellie suspected Marian lacked. Ellie wondered why on earth she let him talk to her that way, then caught sight of Marian's eyes as they rested on Tony and suddenly knew. Poor girl. She loved him. It was hard to discern any symptoms of love for Marian in the senior park ranger.

They had a pleasant day. Ellie looked over the ranger station, studying their collection of photographs and the maps of the park. They took a walk to some falls where they ate the picnic lunch that Simon had provided, and by the end of the day Ellie felt as if she had known them all forever. If anyone was the odd man out it was Simon, who had known them far longer. Ellie could see that he hadn't as much to say to them as she had. He didn't share their interests.

Marian walked beside Ellie as they made their way back to the ranger station, and they had so much to talk about that they fell behind the men.

'It's lovely to have a woman to talk to,' Marian said shyly. 'I mean, the boys are great, but it's not the same.'

Ellie understood. As nice as men were, there was still nothing like having another woman around. She guessed that Marian felt rather lonely at times here.

'I know,' said Ellie encouragingly. 'There are things you can't say to them. They seem nice, though — Tony and JB.'

Marian nodded. 'They are. Tony—his bark's worse than his bite. He—he doesn't really mean the things he says, you know.'

Ellie smiled. 'I know. There's a lot of kindness underneath that gruff exterior.'

Marian nodded. 'There is. Or I wouldn't l—like him.'

'You do care for him, don't you?' said Ellie gently.

Again Marian nodded, this time rather miserably, Ellie thought.

'He—he doesn't know I exist in that way, of course. I'm just one of the boys to him.'

Her statement echoed Ellie's earlier thought, but even as she heard the girl say it Ellie wondered. Did he? Tony was another species again. And perhaps his courtship rituals were different from other people's.

'Perhaps he's slow to notice things,' she suggested. 'It may come to him in time that you're *not* one of them.'

Marian gave a low chuckle, and Ellie was pleased to see her customary cheerfulness reassert itself.

'You do make me feel better, Ellie. I hope we'll see you often.'

'I do like them,' Ellie said to Simon as they drove away down the mountain. 'Especially Marian.'

'Yes? A little insipid, I think,' he replied.

'Oh, no, she's not, Simon! Just shy!'

Simon shrugged a shoulder. 'She won't get Gallagher any way, no matter how much she chases him.'

Ellie stared at him in indignation. What a rotten thing to say! Marian didn't chase him! His tone had been harshly unsympathetic. Ellie wondered suddenly if Simon had been bored at the park, and whether the remark was born of petulance. He hadn't been the centre of attention today.

'She'd suit Charlie,' he added. 'He likes her. And she's just as big a klutz as he is.'

Since it was a term Ellie had used in relation to Charlie herself, it was perhaps surprising that she felt so indignant. But she did. She wondered whether Simon's charm was just a façade. Underneath it, she suspected he had some rather unlovable qualities. He was arrogant and patronising and unsympathetic. Charlie might be vague and clumsy, and the Lord knew what kind of anaesthetist he was, but he was *kind*. She couldn't say that of Simon just now.

Ellie kept her peace. It would do no good to argue. She suspected it would only make him more bad-tempered.

CHAPTER FOUR

MAY was a lovely month in Australia, Ellie thought as she strolled over to Casualty in the morning. The punishing heat of summer was gone, along with the rains of March and April. Clear, sunny days followed one another, with just enough of coolness in the air to make you feel energetic. It was pleasant to have breakfast with cheerful companions and the sun streaming through the long windows. Simon had regained his good humour, and had been smiling and cheerful this morning.

In the corridor leading to Cas, she met Edna, the cleaner, emerging from Charlie Carmody's office opposite.

'There! I've cleaned and tidied it from top to bottom!' she said with satisfaction.

Ellie grinned. 'Will he complain about not being able to find anything, Edna?'

Edna leaned on her mop. 'To tell you the truth, love, I don't think 'e even notices.'

It drew a laugh from Ellie. She said she could well believe it.

'Mind you,' said Edna, screwing up her shrewd eyes, 'it's funny what 'e will notice sometimes.'

Ellie began work in an optimistic mood that was only slightly disturbed at morning tea by Caroline.

'Are you and Simon going to the mess dinner at Bega Hospital?' she asked. No question could more clearly have shown Ellie in what light her friendship with the doctor was viewed by others. People were beginning to regard them as a pair.

She felt a stab of irritation. Really, she'd dined with him three times, lunched with him once and spent a day in the park. What right did they have to assume what they did? But she knew that much of it was due to Simon. He made no secret of his interest. She knew a need to distance herself from him, to declare her independence. She wasn't going to be railroaded into anything, attractive as he might be.

'He hasn't asked me,' she replied lightly.

'Oh, well, it's weeks away yet. He hasn't got round to it,' said Caroline placidly.

Ellie tried again, more directly. 'We're just friends, you know, Caroline.'

'Oh,' was her reply, and Ellie thought she'd never heard one less convinced.

But there was no more time to think about it, for the next moment came the phone call from ambulance control. There had been a car accident on the highway. Three casualities. One bad. He was still in the car, pinned against the wheel. They were cutting him out.

Ellie swung into the well-ordered routines she had used so often at Royal North Shore. She spoke to Sister in Medical and soon had an extra, rather nervous nurse. She dealt quickly with the patients that were there, encouraging Peter to do the same, to clear the decks. She set up around three beds drip sets, blood-taking apparatus, suture packs, dressings. She readied the resuscitation trolley, charged the defibrillator, set up another trolley with gear for insertion of a chest tube. If the man was crushed against the steering-wheel, chances were they would need it. All the time, she gave quiet encouragement to the others, with an eye on their reactions. She saw today why Caroline hadn't wanted her job. The older nurse was jittery. But Ellie understood, and she knew how to steady her.

Finally she rang the other departments — Haematology, X-Ray and Biochem — to let them know that she might need their services in a hurry. When she finished, Pete came to the phone, brushing his hair back with a nervous hand. She heard him talk to Charlie Carmody, and saw him replace the receiver with relief.

'It's OK,' he said. 'Charlie can come when we need him. They've finished that big op.'

'That's good,' said Ellie. 'There's Simon, too. I asked Sister to let him know.'

'Oh, yeah,' said Pete, and swept his eyes round the room, to start when the outside phone rang again.

Ellie saw over his shoulder what he wrote on the pad on the desk. Forty-five-year-old female — scalp laceration, leg fractures. Fourteen-year-old female — bruises, shock. So far, not bad. Then, forty-six-year-old male — head injuries, chest injuries, query abdominal injuries, limb fractures. That was the one that would require all their expertise.

'The mother and the daughter are on their way,' Pete told her. 'It's a family. Skidded off the road. The bloke's still trapped. The others'll be here in fifteen.'

Ellie cast her eye over her preparations once more with the additional information in mind, but could think of nothing to add. So she went to the urn at the end of the ward, and rapidly made four cups of tea. 'Here you are, you lot!' she called. 'You might not get another for a while.'

Gratefully they came and stood together, sipping at the tea. This sort of thing was steadying, and for fifteen long minutes there was nothing they could do. Only one more task did Ellie perform. She called the social worker. The teenage daughter might need her more than them.

The waiting was always awful, no matter how experienced you were. It was a relief when finally the ambulances were heard and the doors to the casualty entrance slammed back. The ambulance officer who had brought in Bessie Lucknow shot the first trolley in through the doors.

'Not too bad, Sis,' he said reassuringly. 'Fractured tib and fib, I reckon, and scalp wound.' They had done their job well. There were inflatable splints on the woman's lower legs and a bandage round her head. 'The kid's just bruised as far as I can tell, Doc,' he said to Pete as the second trolley appeared. Even so, Ellie was glad to see that Simon had come down to help Pete. Pete had been looking a little pale himself.

Together they transferred their charges to the beds, and the sequence of caring for trauma patients unfolded in the prescribed way. Check airway and chest first. No breath—no life. Then circulation—pulse, blood-pressures, find the bleeding, stop it. Then the cerebrum—check for serious head injury, for level of consciousness. Then the spine, the abdomen, the limbs.

There were no surprises here. The ambo was right. The girl—Suzie—was only bruised and numbed with shock. The mother would be all right. They gave her morphine. Simon put a drip in, took blood to check her haemoglobin. Pete sewed up the scalp wound. They X-rayed her legs. In the midst of it, Ellie had another call from ambulance control. The casualty was free. ETA fifteen.

Ellie relayed the message to the doctors. Confirmed head, chest, lower limbs. Probable abdo.

'Charlie know about this?' asked Simon, frowning.

'Yes.'

'Well, better get him,' he said casually.

Ellie was surprised to see Pete look relieved. What was he worried about with Simon there already? He was a nervous Nellie.

Ellie worked to keep things running smoothly and to prepare for the more serious casualty. She saw Suzie cleared by Simon to go off with the social worker, wrapped in a blanket. She helped the nurses tidy away round the bed of the mother.

'Here are your X-rays!' she called as the runner dumped them in her hands.

Charlie Carmody strolled into Cas as she stuck them on the screens, and as the first wail of the siren was heard. They had not used the sirens bringing the first two in. This time the boys were in a hurry.

Pete babbled at Charlie the list of injuries of the incoming patient, but Ellie wondered if he had heard. He was gazing calmly and with interest at the X-rays, not one bit different from the way he normally was. He was in his theatre pyjamas, and only looked larger than usual, with huge, muscled arms and a powerful neck.

'Bilateral compound tib and fib,' he said. 'Front-seat passenger. They'll need to be pinned.'

Ellie heard the siren die at the entrance, and the slamming of doors, and then Pete's muttered, 'Jesus!' as they shot the trolley in. She saw Charlie briefly grip the young doctor's shoulder, and Simon, oddly, standing back, so that it was Charlie who stepped up to the mangled mess transferred in seconds to the bed.

Two hours ago, Robert Coutts had been enjoying a holiday with his wife and child. Now he was barely alive. He was unconscious, blood from head to foot. His face was a pupled, misshapen mass, the eyes closed by swelling and full of more blood. The bandage round his head was soaked in it. His chest, hardly moving, was covered in it. It oozed from a dozen lacerations and stuck his trouser legs to his shattered limbs. He was one of those casualties where Ellie couldn't see how the doctors knew where to start. And he was dying fast.

Ellie jerked her eyes to Charlie. How could slow, bumbling Charlie cope with this? Why didn't Simon move in? Charlie stood immobile, just looking. Oh, God! Ellie groaned inside herself.

But then, all at once, he did move. And Ellie saw before her astonished eyes a transformation. For slow, vague Charlie Carmody swung into action like a high-powered machine, with orders so rapid and movements so fast that for a moment she was left behind, her wits scattered.

'Get a drip in, Simon. Hand me scissors. Chest tube first. Cross-match twelve units. Slide match six. BP monitor on. Run in the fluid, fast as it'll go.' He spoke calmly, but fast, and as he spoke he worked, as quickly and surely as he thought. He cut the man's clothing from his chest himself, and in seconds had determined, 'Tension pneumothorax here. Let's get a chest tube in fast.'

Ellie had moved round to assist. She knew what it meant. Robert Coutts' ribs had been smashed up like matchwood, lacerating his lungs. The right one had collapsed. The oxygen he was breathing was pouring into his chest cavity, squashing the lung down even further, pushing the heart over and stopping it from filling. He was in deep trouble.

Charlie began the procedure to insert a tube through the wall of his chest, to drain out the air. Ellie had never seen a doctor work so fast. He was like lightning. Usually she was ahead of them, waiting with what they wanted next. But today she barely kept up. He had cut down into the chest cavity before she had time to strip the tube from its sterile wrapping.

'I'm sorry!' she gasped as he waited, and was amazed, when she flicked her eyes up, to see him actually smile.

'You're doing wonderfully,' he said with unimpaired calm.

Ellie was staggered. But there was no time to think about it. Charlie didn't stop. Chest tube, endotracheal tube down his windpipe, blood sucked out of the mouth, another drip, more fluids, blood transfusion, exploration of the head wound, examination of the whole body. Task after task, performed with a cool virtuosity that Ellie had never seen matched, till order was produced out of chaos.

'OK, we're getting organised here,' he said quietly to the other doctors. 'One of you could attend to the wife now.'

'I'll do it,' said Simon. 'Pete can learn more here.' Ellie thought he sounded pleased to go.

Still Charlie worked, his gaze sweeping the patient, the monitors, the staff as they followed his orders. Ellie lifted her face to look at his in a momentary lull, and saw there not one trace of his customary vagueness. The grey eyes were keen as lasers.

He took new problems in his stride. 'He's coning,' he said. 'Let's do a craniotomy.'

Ellie had only seen one before. It was a horrendous thing to have to undertake in Cas. Robert Coutts was bleeding inside his head. The expanding blood clot was pressing on the brain, beginning to force it down the opening in the base of the skull. It would kill him, quickly. Charlie had to make a hole in his skull, to pick the broken pieces of bone out of the brain, and release the blood.

Feverishly, Ellie threw together what he needed. Could she remember? But already his calm voice was in her ears, helping, steadying. They gowned, and she watched him perform the delicate procedure effortlessly, all clumsiness gone.

Ellie had a sense of disbelief when it was over. She slumped into a chair beside the other nurses and Pete, and surveyed the wreckage of her casualty department. It looked as though a bomb had gone off. Not only had Charlie had to do a craniotomy, but he had opened the patient's abdomen as well to stop the bleeding from his liver.

He had done it, and over the hours Robert Coutts had been dragged back from the brink of death to a state where he was stable enough to be flown to Canberra by chopper to have complicated surgery on his legs. He would make it. No one knew how bad the head injury was, and how he would end up, but he had a chance.

'Holy cow!' breathed Caroline, and they all laughed suddenly with relief. 'I suppose they do this sort of thing every day at North Shore,' she added.

'Like hell they do!' exclaimed Ellie. 'I've seen one craniotomy, and two emergency laparotomies. But I've never seen anyone do them all, one after another, as if — as if they were paring corns!'

They all burst out laughing again. 'Yeah. He's bloody amazing, isn't he?' said Caroline.

Pete shook his head, and said what he'd said once before. 'He's great! There's just no one like him.'

As Ellie began the weary task of cleaning up so that they could get on with the ordinary work, she couldn't help but agree. She was still astonished. She had put him down as a bumbler, nice but dim. Now she realised that his preoccupied air must come from absorption in his thoughts. For this man had shown he possessed a mind like a razor, as well as nerves of steel. It had been an extraordinary performance — of intellect, knowledge, resolution and calmness, as well as of the surest pair of hands she had ever seen.

And to think she had wished for Simon to step in! Simon had acted with wisdom. He knew his limitations. There was no way he could compete with Charlie's talent for resuscitation. It was little short of genius.

'Yippee! Sandwiches!' called Caroline, and Ellie suddenly realised she was starving. It was three-thirty, and they hadn't had lunch. But she went on working.

'You start,' she called back. Ellie would stop only when Cas was ready to receive another just like the last. By the time she had finished setting up the resuscitation trolley again, the others had finished and gone back to their patients.

Ellie made herself a cup of tea, and sat down at the desk. She had devoured three sandwiches in record time, thinking, Saving lives makes you hungry, when Charlie strolled back through the door. He was in a new set of surgical pyjamas. The last ones had been covered in blood.

Ellie was aware of an odd new shyness. Something made her get to her feet. 'Would — would you like a cup of tea, Dr Carmody?' she said, and wondered immediately what had made her call him that. Even the cleaners called him Charlie.

His slow smile dawned, a little rueful. 'Don't you trust me with the urn, Ellie?' he asked.

Ellie gave a choke of laughter and at the same time blushed. 'No! It's not that! I just thought — I'll make one for you.'

His smile was now a grin. 'No,' he said. 'Go on with your lunch. I'll make one myself. You can keep me in sight.'

Another chuckle escaped her, but the shyness didn't abate. She knew what it was. Simon had treated him as something of a joke, and that was how she'd thought of him. Now she knew there was no one in the world more worthy of respect. And her new respect was even tinged with a little awe. How could she have laughed at him? It occurred to her suddenly that Simon's treatment of him might well stem from jealousy.

The smile still lurked in his eyes as he brought his cup of tea to her desk and arranged his powerful form beside her in a chair. Ellie knew the urge to study this enigmatic man anew. Her eyes traced the lines of the large hands, recently so deft, and the great, muscled forearms and powerful biceps. She realised, flushing, that she hadn't offered him a sandwich, and did so now. 'The others have eaten,' she said. 'I've had enough.' She wanted to say something about how wonderful he'd been, but couldn't find the words. And then she was embarrassed to find he was congratulating her.

'I was too slow for you,' she said.

But he shook his head. 'You were faster than anyone I've worked with before.'

'I wonder how that poor little kid's getting on?' she said, partly to change the subject.

'Not too badly, considering,' he said. 'I looked in on her. To explain things.'

How typically kind, Ellie thought. Not many consultants would have thought of that. They'd have been content for the social worker to relay information. But Ellie suddenly knew that it was more than information he'd gone to give. It was comfort too. And she couldn't think of anyone who would be more comforting.

'That was nice,' she said softly, and thought he looked a little embarrassed.

'I don't know how Robert will do — brain-wise,' he said. 'It may be weeks or months before we know.'

'He's got a chance,' she said.

He turned to her and smiled, a trifle sadly. 'Yes,' he said, and began absently to destroy his polystyrene cup. There was a long pause, then, 'Do you like it here?' he asked suddenly.

Ellie met his gaze and gave her lilting smile. 'I love it here,' she said with perfect truthfulness.

He held her eyes for a moment, his own warm. 'That's good.' He looked away again, apparently stuck for something more to say, and completed his demolition of the cup. Then he looked up abruptly, his face alert. 'What time is it?' he asked.

'Four o'clock,' said Ellie.

Charlie gave a small groan. 'I think I'm meant to be somewhere else,' he said guiltily.

Ellie grinned to herself five minutes later when she was able to tell an irate Paul Vassy that Charlie was on his way. Charlie hadn't changed.

'Aren't you going home?' asked Simon at five-thirty. 'Your shift finished an hour ago.'

'We got behind, with that trauma,' she explained. 'I can't leave the evening staff with all this.'

'They'll cope,' he said impatiently. 'It's only a few minor matters.'

'And three more still in the waiting area,' she told him. 'What's the hurry?'

'I thought you might come for a plate of pasta with me.'

'Oh. No, Simon, not tonight. I'm tired.' Ellie knew it was a lie. But she didn't feel able to tell him the truth in the middle of Cas. The truth was she didn't want to see him that often. She hadn't forgotten her conversation with Caroline earlier that day.

'You need a massage,' he said, putting up his hands to knead the muscles of her shoulders in full view of everyone in Cas.

'Don't, Simon,' she protested, and she saw a spark of anger spring up in his eyes. 'Go on. Have a tantrum,' she said, and he suddenly gave a shout of laughter that made Ellie laugh, too.

'You're a darling,' he said, and pulled her against him for a moment in a hug. 'All right. I'm going. Hello, Charlie,' he said over her head. 'Finished in Theatre?'

Ellie knew a sudden feeling of dismay that Charlie had seen that. She didn't approve herself of public displays of affection between staff. But Charlie looked unmoved when she reluctantly turned to face him.

'Yes. Paul's fixed up Eve Coutts' legs,' he said, more to Ellie than Simon. 'Looks like a nice job.' Ellie was glad to see him smile as benignly as ever. 'Suzie's up with her now.'

'That's good,' Ellie said, and managed a smile in return.

'I think Pete wants me,' he said.

'Does he? He's in the second cubicle.'

Charlie ambled away. 'Do you have to hug me in Cas in front of the med super?' Ellie asked Simon.

He grinned. 'Don't worry about it. Charlie won't have noticed. He doesn't know women are different,' he said cheekily as he strolled to the door.

CHAPTER FIVE

ELLIE resisted Simon Taverner's considerable powers of persuasion for the remainder of the week, agreeing only to join the crowd from Medical once more for Sunday lunch. It was a pleasant part of Australian life to lunch with friends in the shelter of the ghost gums in the pub garden. Simon took it well enough, accepting her reiteration that she only wanted to be friends with nothing more than a superior smile.

Now that she had seen Charlie Carmody in a different light, she began to notice a number of things about him that she hadn't noticed before. One was the confidence that others seemed to place in his opinions. Paul Vassy often asked for his advice as they sat together at breakfast or dinner. Even Simon sometimes sought his opinion, though Ellie had the feeling that it was not something he relished doing. To the housemen and nursing staff of the Base, there was evidently no higher authority.

Watching him in Cas, she began to realise that it didn't take long for him to gain the patients' implicit trust. There was something so solid and reassuring about him. He listened. And he explained. He never made them feel they were too ignorant to understand. Ellie could see why they liked him, and why, in the case of some regular patients who knew him well, the feeling came close to love. Old ladies like Bessie Lucknow put all their faith in him when they were sick, and began to mother him when they felt well again. It was Charlie who received presents of fresh home-made scones and hand-knitted socks after those he had cared for had gone home.

'More socks for you, Charlie!' said Caroline Tuckey, snooping into a parcel left at the casualty desk. 'Your patients must think you're a centipede!'

Charlie gave his good-natured rumbling laugh, and came to look, reading the note of thanks pinned to the parcel. 'That's kind of her,' he said warmly. 'Irene Ford.'

'Whaddya do with all them socks, Charlie?' asked Barney, the porter.

'Oh, they come in handy,' he said. 'I seem to be forever losing one of a pair.'

'Where do they go, I wonder?' asked Ellie musingly, her head on one side. 'Sixteen million people in Australia. Let's say they all lose only two socks a year. That means somewhere there are thirty-two million stray socks!'

There was a shout of laughter. Charlie Carmody grinned down at her. 'They're with the umbrellas,' he suggested.

Ellie gave a ripple of a laugh. 'Well, I hope wherever they are they're having a nice time.'

It also dawned on Ellie that Charlie was *never* vague or clumsy when he was working, emergency or not. He might lean against a bedside table and knock the patient's water jug over when the patient was a farmer he knew and he'd come for a chat, but in his work he was always precise and dextrous. Ellie didn't mind how many water jugs he knocked over, as long as he was always on hand for the urgent cases.

On Thursday they had another road casualty — this time a motor-cyclist who'd come off his bike on the Berringar road. When the ambulance officers brought him in with blood spurting from the severed artery in his thigh, Ellie was glad that Charlie was there. The young man had lost enough blood for his blood-pressure to be getting low.

'I'd wear gloves for this one, Doc,' said the ambulance man. 'Reckon he's on the needle. We found these in his backpack while we were looking for his ID.' He held out the unmistakable equipment of the drug addict.

They all knew what that meant. The patient might have hepatitis, or even AIDS. Ellie hurried to provide them all with the gloves and plastic goggles which would protect them from the patients's blood, and got out the red 'Infection Risk' labels that would go on any samples they took from him.

'Stand back, Ellie,' Charlie said, when he had analgesia and fluids running into the boy's veins and was ready to tackle the wound. 'This will spurt when I take the packs off.'

It did. The major artery of the thigh was cut in the deep laceration, and he still had sufficient blood-pressure for a few jets of blood to spray over Charlie's chest and neck before he got the clamp on. It was soon controlled, however, and smaller bleeders clamped, and the wound repacked to hold him till he got to Theatre. There, Paul Vassy would cut out the damaged flesh and try to rejoin the major nerves and vessels.

'He needs blood before Paul starts on him,' said Charlie. 'That fluid will keep his pressure up for a while, but he needs three units before Theatre.'

'It's on its way,' said Pete.

Charlie stripped off his gloves and threw them in the 'Contaminated' bag that Ellie had provided.

Ellie turned to Caroline. 'Caroline, can you get Charlie a clean surgical top, please?' she asked. Everything smeared with this man's blood had to go in the yellow bag.

'Thank you.' Charlie smiled, and carefully pulled off his top so that the blood didn't come into contact with his face, then dropped it in after the gloves.

'Have you got any on you?' she asked, turning to inspect him, and then found herself brought up short by the sight before her.

'Not much,' he said, 'and I've go no cuts.'

But it wasn't the blood that had soaked through his shirt that made her stand and stare. It was the figure of Charlie Carmody. She thought she had never seen anything more magnificent. He stood facing her, as tall and straight as a tree, and about as big. If he looked like a mammoth of a man with his clothes on, that was nothing to the way he looked with them off. In fact, she reflected, you had to see him that way really to appreciate the scale on which he was built.

He wasn't fat. He was just built like a bulldozer. His powerful neck surmounted a pair of massive shoulders and a broad chest on which the muscles stood out in perfect curves. A light dusting of dark hair adorned it, and continued down in a faint line across the taut, flat belly. Ellie's eyes took in the further details of bulging biceps and forearms like two Christmas hams.

Barney, lounging against a bench in case he was needed, voiced her thoughts for her. 'Bloody hell, Charlie. You are a big boy, aren't you? Do you work out?'

Charlie shook his head, looking embarrassed. 'No. I think my mother just fed me too well.'

Ellie gave a little breathless gust of laughter. It had been such a shock, seeing him like that. It had thrown her off balance, somehow.

Caroline's voice came from the end of the room.

'The biggest top we've got is large.' She held it up. 'I don't think it's going to do it.'

It certainly didn't. Ellie collected her wits. 'Barney, could you be a pal, and get Charlie an extra-large top from Theatre?'

'Sure thing,' he said, and cracked a joke as he slouched away. 'I wouldn't like to be disobliging to a bloke built like that.'

Ellie ran a cloth under the hot tap and squeezed it out. 'Do you want to wash the blood off?' she asked, and held it out to him.

He peered down. It was mostly high up on his chest, with some on his neck. 'Can you see it all?' he asked. She could see that he couldn't.

Ellie swallowed and nodded. He stepped up to the sink, and as unconcernedly as she could she wiped the blood stains from his body. But it felt very strange to be standing so close to him like this, performing such an intimate service. Ever so slightly, her hand shook as she gently sponged off the last of it, and handed him some paper towel on which to dry himself.

He took it, saying, 'Thank you. Service above the call of duty,' and smiled down at her warmly.

It drew an answering smile from her, but she was aware of an uncomfortable tension, and was glad to go and answer the phone. 'That blood'll be ten more minutes,' she told Charlie as he came to sit on the desk by her.

'Good,' he said. 'I'll ring Surgical and let Paul know what's in store.'

Ellie bent her head to pen her admission notes as he did so, but found that she couldn't stop her eyes from straying to him. There was somethng very disturbing about having him sitting before her bare like that. It made her tense and awkward.

She scrawled her signature at the bottom of her notes as he put the phone down, got up at the same moment he did and collided with him.

He put his hands on her shoulders to steady her, and smiled apologetically. 'I'm sorry,' he said.

'No, it was my fault,' she replied quickly, her throat oddly constricted. She felt a flush stealing over her cheeks.

'No one else would say that,' he said. 'I've been told I take up too much room.'

Ellie gave a little spurt of laughter, and looked up with her impish grin. 'Oh, well. At least you're not a *waste* of space, Dr Carmody, like some people I could name.'

He gave a delighted shout of laughter and spontaneously hugged her to his side. 'Kind Ellie!' she heard him say, feeling his deep voice rumbling in his chest. But she couldn't bring herself to reply. She was too floored by the feel of it, and just by the fact of being pressed to his nakedness.

He seemed to realise the awkwardness of it himself. He dropped his arm, and they parted quickly. 'I'm sorry,' he said, a trifle breathlessly. 'I didn't think.'

Ellie felt a little giddy, and searched for a light reply. She was very glad to be spared the necessity when Barney reappeared with the top.

'Here yer go, boss,' he said. 'I hope yer haven't caught yer death, delicate flower as you are,' and the awkwardness was gratefully lost in laughter.

'God, he's a beautiful beast, isn't he?' said Caroline when Charlie and the patient had gone to Theatre. 'He can stand around here all day with his shirt off if he likes.'

Ellie smiled. 'I thought you were happily married?' she asked quizzically.

'I can look, can't I?' grinned Caroline. 'I wonder why nobody's snapped him up?'

'I wonder,' repeated Ellie musingly. But she didn't wonder long. There was a child with a broken arm, a man with a deep splinter, a bee sting, a sprained ankle, and a woman with chest pain to think about. And that was only in the next hour.

It wasn't till she stood gratefully under the shower at the end of the day that she had time to wonder again. Caroline was right. He was a magnificent animal, and as nice a man as you'd ever meet to boot. He must be approaching mid-thirties. Why wasn't he married? She would bet her life that he wasn't of the other persuasion. She rememberd what Simon had said on the way back from Goolcoola—that Charlie liked Marian. Maybe that meant more than she had thought at the time. She knew a sudden stab of sadness at the thought.

That would be awful, She didn't want to think of Charlie being locked in an eternal triangle with Tony and Marian. He was too nice to suffer like that, she told herself. She hoped for his sake that it wasn't so.

And what a waste it would be for the women of the world, she thought with a smile. For a moment her mind darted back to that friendly moment when he'd hugged her. It had been rather embarrassing, of course. That was why her heart had speeded up, and she'd felt so strange. Poor Charlie. He'd been embarrassed, too. He'd done it before he'd remembered he wasn't dressed for friendly hugs. But she couldn't deny that it had also felt nice to lean against the warm, hard smoothness of his chest. Yes, it would be a waste for Charlie to be in love with Marian. Plenty of other women would be pleased to snap him up.

* * *

'You're quiet today,' Simon remarked. 'Not working too hard, are you?'

'Hardly,' Ellie replied, taking a sip of her beer. 'Just feeling lazy. It's nice here in the sun.'

'Too much roast pork?' suggested Garry, the house-man from Medical.

'Yes, probably,' she agreed.

'That's the trouble with this pub,' Garry said. 'The food's too good. If I keep coming here on a Sunday, I'll have to let my trousers out.'

It was true. The food was excellent—plain country fare, but well-cooked and rather too much of it. But Ellie knew that was not why she was quiet. The truth was she was rather bored.

It surprised her. There was plenty of talk, and Simon, as always, was cheerful and full of wit. It was just that she was beginning to feel she'd heard it all before. He seemed to have nothing new to say. There was a lot of shop, which she got sick of. And a lot of friendly joking and ribbing. But none of this lot seemed to have anything serious to say, or any different topics to talk about.

'Have you got any hobbies, Simon?' she asked with sudden curiosity, and immediately felt rather foolish for blurting out the question. But this crew could turn anything into a joke.

'He has,' said Mark, the surgical houseman, 'but he'd be silly to tell you about them.'

There was a general laugh, in which Simon joined, but he quickly added, 'All in the past. You know that, Staunton.' He turned to her. 'What sort of things did you have in mind?'

'Oh, I don't know. Anything.' Ellie could feel herself blushing.

He grinned. 'You mean, like breeding animals?' he

asked teasingly. She shrugged. 'No. I leave that sort of thing to the eccentrics of this world,' he said.

It annoyed her. Charlie wasn't eccentric. He was doing something that mattered. She was glad when Mark Staunton spoke up in Charlie's defence.

'I think it's great what he's doing, actually. We're going to lose those species if someone doesn't do something about them. He know heaps about it, too.'

Ellie thought Simon looked rather annoyed. Nor was he quite able to keep an edge of irritation out of his voice when he replied, 'What's one species of possum more or less?'

'Simon! Where does that argument end?' Ellie cried.

He shrugged. 'I really don't care. The topic bores me, actually.'

Ellie bit back the words that rose to her tongue. They were, Well, you bore *me*! But she suddenly knew it was true. It was a revelation. Simon *did* bore her — because he was narrow, and self-centred, and closed-minded. The realisation was so surprising, it deprived her of speech. The heart-throb of the hospital, and he bored her! She almost laughed out loud.

'I don't have time for hobbies,' he said. 'I have enough to do keeping this crowd in order.' And with that the banter began again.

Charlie was in his usual spot on a late Sunday afternoon when Ellie returned. He looked up from the book he was reading when she came into the common-room, and smiled.

'Have you had a cup of tea?' she asked politely. 'I'm going to make one.'

'I didn't dare,' he said ruefully. 'It's a new jug.'

She gave a peal of laughter. 'Oh, no! Charlie! It can't be true!'

He grinned. 'No. I'm lying. For sympathy. I hadn't got round to it yet.'

'I'll make you one,' she offered.

'I was angling for that, too,' he confessed, and Ellie began to see that what Bessie Lucknow had said was true. Charlie knew how to pull your leg.

Ellie grinned as she put the cup down on the arm of his chair. 'Here,' she said, then caught sight of what he was reading. 'Oh! Do you like poetry?' It was a book of Australian poems.

'Mmm. Some.'

'Whose are you reading?' she asked shyly.

'Banjo Patterson.'

Ellie smiled.'"The Man from Snowy River". "Clancy of the Overflow".'

He smiled back. 'Yes. The old favourites. Do you like them?'

She nodded. 'Especially "The Man from Snowy River".'

He handed her the book. 'Read it to me.'

'Oh, no!' Ellie blushed scarlet. 'I couldn't.' She handed the book back. 'Do you—do you feel like reading it?' she asked. 'I love to hear it read aloud.'

He smiled again and nodded, turning to the page. Ellie settled herself on the ottoman in front of his chair, and rested her chin on her hands.

She had never heard it read better. He was just the man to do it—a big, strong man with a deep, resonant voice, ideal for a tale of hard riding and heroism in the Australian bush. The hairs stood up on the back of her neck at the climax as they always did when she heard it read well.

'Thank you,' she said at the end, 'that was wonderful,' and added quickly, because she could see she'd embarrassed him, 'Do you ride?'

'Yes. Not often now. But I grew up in the country. In the Southern Tablelands.'

'Oh. Was your family on the land?'

He nodded. 'Beef cattle and sheep.'

'What made you become a doctor?' she asked curiously. 'Didn't you want to farm?'

'N-no. Too narrow a life. Too restricting. I have a brother who was willing to carry on, luckily. I thought of being a vet for a while.'

'Why didn't you?' she asked. 'You like animals.'

His smile broadened. 'I quite like people, too,' he said with a twinkle, 'and —' the smile receded a little, became a little sad ' — people are so much more aware of their suffering than other animals. With their big brains, they apprehend their own misery so keenly. And, with their love for each other, when one suffers, many do.'

Ellie regarded him silently, her chin still propped on her hands. His quiet speech had caught at her heart. She felt her eyes mist. It was about the best reason for doing medicine she'd ever heard.

He saw, and a look of concern filled his face. 'I'm sorry!' he said. 'I didn't mean to make you sad!'

Ellie bent her head, embarrassed to be so emotional, but he had slid forward in his chair and, placing his big hands either side of her head, with infinite gentleness he lifted her face to his.

'I'm sorry,' he said again. 'I've upset you.' The grey eyes looked tenderly into hers.

'No — I — no. It's not that. You didn't. It's just that it's so true — what you said. I'm not sad.' She gave him a smile to prove it.

He smiled back at her, his good-humoured mouth curving upwards and his eyes warm. He *was* beautiful,

she thought suddenly. Inside *and* out. Ellie felt a
sudden rush of affection for him. Dear, kind Charlie.

'Do you want to see what the possums are up to?' he
asked. 'It's just dark. They'll be awake now, expecting
dinner.' Ellie readily agreed.

Outside, he gave her an upturned feed-pail to sit on
and squatted down beside her. 'She has three seasons
a year,' he told her. 'She could have three offspring a
year if we were lucky. But she hasn't accepted either
of them as a mate yet. She's just playing.'

'What's her name?' asked Ellie.

'I haven't named her, or the other male,' he admitted. 'Would you like to?'

Ellie grinned. 'I think we should call *her* Jezebel!'

He gave his deep laugh. 'Jezebel. Yes. That's good.
What about him?'

The young possum was sidling around the female,
playfully nudging her, attempting to gain her interest.
'Casanova,' Ellie said, and heard Charlie laugh again.
'What do you feed them?' she asked, and they sat for
a long while, watching the possums eating, and talking
of them and a dozen other things. One topic seemed to
lead to another.

'Watch this. This is dessert,' said Charlie, taking
some grapes out of a bag. He placed them just inside
the door of the enclosure. 'Are you cold?' he asked.

'Not yet,' she replied, but didn't mind when he put
his arm around her and hugged her to the warmth of
his side. They watched the old possum, Hercules,
discover that the grapes were there.

'He doesn't miss much,' Charlie said, his breath
warm in her hair.

Hercules was worth watching. In much the way a
human would, he held a grape in one little hand and
brought it to his mouth. Ellie would almost have sworn

his eyes lit up when he tasted it. He then munched at it so avidly and so noisily that Ellie had to laugh.

'He loves it!' she exclaimed.

'Yes, they're a favourite,' Charlie agreed, and the others came scampering over to bear out the truth of his words. Quite a free-for-all ensued, with three possums grabbing grapes in both hands and pushing them into their little faces as fast as they possibly could.

'It's so funny!' Ellie said, giggling, and looked up at him. 'They *are* beautiful. It would be awful if they were to disappear.'

Charlie smiled down at her and gave her a friendly answering squeeze — and suddenly Ellie felt herself tremble beneath his arm. A tight, hot sweetness seemed to seize her, and the breath to catch in her throat.

'You *are* cold,' he said, and put his other arm around her, enveloping her against his chest.

But she hadn't been cold. It was something else. And now it was even worse. Ellie felt Charlie's body against her, large and warm and hard. She felt his heart beating in his chest with a powerful, even beat. And in herself she felt a fierce, exciting current of desire.

She had felt nothing like it before. It seemed to electrify her. She longed to turn to him, to press herself closer against him, to find his mouth with her own.

'We'd better get you inside,' he said.

'Yes,' she said tightly. Yes. Please! Poor Charlie! What would he do if he knew what she was feeling? She thought he would die of embarrassment!

Ellie splashed her face with water in the bathroom before going in to dinner. How extraordinary that she should feel like that! She had been stirred by his physical presence in a way she had never been with anyone else. Her mind went back to Charlie without his shirt on, and she had to admit that she had felt the first current of it then. He was such a fine physical specimen. Perhaps it was not surprising that he'd drawn from her a biological response.

Oh, well. It was nothing to worry about. It only meant she was healthy.

CHAPTER SIX

'DRAW up ten milligrams of morphine and five of Valium, please, Vanessa,' Ellie said. She taped over the cannula Pete had just placed in the middle-aged farmer's hand so that it wouldn't come out.

'We'll give you some morphine to kill the pain, Mr Rowe. And some Valium to relax the muscles round your shoulder, so I can get it back in,' Pete explained. 'It still might hurt a bit, though.'

'It couldn't hurt any worse than it does now!' Jim Rowe said through clenched teeth. Jim had fallen off his tractor and dislocated his shoulder.

Five minutes later he lay half asleep. His arm was still held at an odd angle, but he no longer appeared to care.

'OK,' said Pete softly. 'We'll have a go now. Charlie's shown me how to do this.' Carefully he grasped the man's wrist and elbow and drew the arm out and down in Kocher's manoeuvre. Jim came awake and gave a goan of pain, but in another moment there was a satisfying clunk as the head of the humerus slipped back into place.

'Great!' said Ellie, and Pete gave a happy grin. The patient gave a great sigh of relief as the pain receded, and fell back into a contented sleep.

'I'll keep an eye on him as he sleeps it off,' Ellie said, and sat on the side of the bed to take his blood-pressure.

Several times that morning, when she'd been left to her own thoughts, her mind had returned to the evening before and those unexpected feelings. She hoped she hadn't betrayed them to Charlie, but thought from his normal comradely demeanour at dinner and breakfast that she hadn't. What was it that Simon had said when he had embraced her in Cas? Charlie wouldn't have noticed. He hadn't realised that women were different. Well, that was stupid, of course. But she didn't think that he had been aware of what his friendly hug in the cold night air had done.

It amused her a little to think that while Simon, with all his efforts, had done nothing for her she had responded to dear, sweet Charlie. It didn't mean anything, of course. She liked him immensely, and admired his enormous competence in medicine. But she thought he was too soft. There were times when Simon was baiting him when she longed to see him lose his temper. It seemed he didn't have a temper to lose. He was just too good-natured. She wondered whether in a way he was a little weak.

He wandered in after lunch and helped Pete with a few things, finally coming to rest at her desk as she filled out some cas cards. 'I spoke to Marian this morning,' he said. 'She asked after you.' There was a short pause. 'She gets a bit lonely up there, I think. Would you like to go up to the park some time?'

Ellie looked up. She did want to go back to Goolcoola, and perhaps take a longer walk. She couldn't see any harm in going with Charlie. It would be nice. 'I'd like to do that,' she said. 'Marian said there were some aboriginal rock carvings at the end of one of the walks.'

He nodded. 'They're good examples,' he said. 'I think they're rather precious. We could go there.' It was settled. They would drive up on Sunday morning.

Ellie found herself looking forward to it through the week.

Her mood was only spoiled a little on Saturday afternoon, when Simon invited her to go with him to the mess dinner which Caroline had mentioned, now two weeks away. It was not easy to refuse with diplomacy, but Ellie knew now that she didn't want to pursue a closer friendship with Simon.

Simon wasn't inclined to take no for an answer. 'Stop worrying about what people will think! What does it matter if they know we're seeing each other?'

Ellie was forced finally to be blunt. 'Simon — I really don't think we've got much in common.'

He stared at her, a look of incomprehension on his face. 'I don't know what you're talking about,' he said.

She sighed inwardly. 'I don't think there's any future in our friendship, Simon.'

His eyebrows rose. Ellie wondered if this was the first time he'd ever been told that. Then she saw the anger gather in his eyes. 'Well, it's a fine time to tell me that, when you've been leading me on for weeks!'

A flush sprang to her cheeks. 'That's not true!' she cried hotly. 'I've said from the start I only wanted to be friends!'

Simon's mouth curled in an ugly sneer. 'I see. It's *your* hobby to make fools of people.'

It wounded her, despite its patent injustice. 'I didn't mean——' she began, but he cut her off.

'You make a sport of teasing!' He had scraped to his feet. 'Well, take care, won't you? Sometimes little flirts like you get more than they bargained for!' And with that he flung outside.

Ellie sat still, her face now pale where it had been flaming. She heard him drive off in his car with a screech of tyres on the asphalt that attested to his temper. She couldn't help it. Two tears rolled down her cheeks. No one had ever said anything like that to her before. She knew it wasn't true, but it still hurt.

'Ellie?' Charlie Carmody's tone of concern came to her from the door of the common-room. Hastily she dashed the tears away with her hand. But he had advanced into the room and dropped down at her side. He covered one of her hands with his own, and began to speak.

Ellie couldn't speak to him. She only wanted to get away. Embarrassed and wounded, she shook her head quickly and got to her feet. 'It's all right,' she managed before she ran away.

When she came down to dinner, she had regained her composure, and was grateful that Charlie didn't refer to the incident again. From his cheerful placidity, one would have thought that he'd forgotten about it. Perhaps he'd decided that it was nothing after all. Ellie was also grateful that Simon didn't return to the Base that night. She went up to bed at eleven, once more looking forward to tomorrow, and didn't see Charlie look at the clock and Simon's empty chair, and frown.

It was with a certain lightness of heart that Ellie climbed into the car beside Charlie the following morning. The feeling grew on her as Charlie guided the car out of the hospital grounds and on to the road to Goolcoola. Ellie leant back comfortably and watched the bush passing, catching glimpses here and there of the vista of sloping hillsides through the trees. The weather was considerably cooler now than when she'd arrived, but the day was sunny. The light filtered down through the treetops, and when they came at last to the entrance road to the park on the top of the plateau the sun shone full on her and made her feel warm and cheerful.

Charlie was a careful driver, she saw. With a certain pleasure she watched his big paws on the wheel. They were large hands, in proportion to the rest of him, but they were well-shaped and sure. He drove as he did most things, as though he had all the time in the world. Ellie found it relaxing, contrary to Paul's prophecy that Charlie's deliberate pace would drive her mad. Simon Taverner drove with much more flair, but there were times when he made her afraid.

Ellie gave a contented sigh. 'This is nice,' she said, and saw Charlie smile.

They were welcomed at the ranger station. She could see that Charlie and the three rangers were firm friends. Marian greeted her with shy pleasure, and Charlie gave Marian a hug.

'You made those sandwiches, Brown?' Tony asked.

'I was just about to,' Marian said, a little flustered.

'Don't!' said Ellie. 'Marje in the hospital kitchen has made us enough to feed ten, and given us a whole cake, too.'

'You've made friends in the right places,' Charlie grinned.

'Oh, she did it for you,' Ellie laughed.

It wasn't long before they set out along the track, fragrant with the eucalupts that grew so thickly that their green canopy let only filtered sunlight through to the ferns and bushes that grew in the under-storey. Ellie fell back beside Marian and let the men go on ahead. Charlie's large khaki-clad figure strode before her at an easy pace, his muscular behind a nice part of the scenery.

She and Marian took up their conversation as though they'd never left off, and in a surprisingly short time they arrived at the edge of a breathtaking drop, where the forest cleared and wide expanses of flat rock were adorned with carvings made perhaps twenty thousand years ago. They explored them in the sunshine, Tony telling them what he knew about them, then sat looking out over the escarpment to eat their lunch.

It was relaxed and friendly, and interesting. Charlie brought out the best in Marian, Ellie noticed. Naturally shy, she seemed perfectly easy with him. Ellie watched him chatting comfortably with her and saw that Marian often laughed and that her pretty round face showed her pleasure. Charlie, too, looked happy in Marian's company. His mouth was curved in a smile and there was a light of gentle humour in his eyes.

Tony told a funny story of their latest experience with the station's temperamental four-wheel drive, in which Marian's lack of mechanical aptitude came in for some satirical comment.

'I don't understand it,' said Tony. 'This is a woman with a university degree who can't even change a tyre.'

'I can!' protested Marian, moved at last to defend herself.

'Yeah, she did once,' observed Tony. 'And twenty miles on the wheel nuts worked themselves loose because she'd put the wheel on the wrong way round.'

There was a laugh in which Marian joined, though her face was red.

'Deny that, Brown,' said Tony drily.

But Charlie showed an inclination to champion her cause. 'Well, at least you did put the wheel nuts on and tighten them. I've forgotten to do both things on occasion.'

Marian gave Charlie a warm look of gratitude. He smiled down at her, and an unmistakably tender light came into his eyes.

All at once Ellie had an odd sensation of disquiet. Simon's statement — 'She'd suit Charlie. He likes her' — and her own past thoughts recurred forcibly. Did Charlie have feelings for Marian that were more than friendly? For some reason the suspicion did not please her at all. Well, that was natural. Marian had said herself that she cared for Tony. Ellie liked Charlie. She didn't want to see him hurt. Ellie went on with her lunch, a little quiet.

'You wondered why we were so pleased to see you, didn't you, Charlie?' said JB. They had returned from their walk and were at the entrance to the park, where a side-road went off the main one. There a dead tree had fallen and was all but blocking the road.

'We'd use the winch on the truck, but it's not working,' Tony said. 'Do you think the three of us could drag it round off the road? Then I can take my time to chop it up with the chain-saw.'

Charlie measured the big old gum with his eyes, and nodded. 'I think so,' he said calmly.

So Marian and Ellie watched as the men rolled up their sleeves. 'Now, Charlie,' said JB, 'we'll just pretend to help you, and you can lift it round.' He turned to Ellie. 'Charlie's dad was a gorilla, you know. He's actually an intelligent half-gorilla.'

Charlie's face broke into a broad grin. 'I'm clumsier than a gorilla,' he admitted. 'Watch out I don't drop it on your foot.'

The three of them lined up, Charlie at the end where the tree was largest and heaviest. The big man bent and hooked his hands under the trunk just above the roots. The others followed suit, and Ellie heard Tony say, 'OK. Ready? Heave!'

Ellie couldn't take her eyes away from Charlie. The

great muscles in his neck and arms bulged and hardened, the veins standing out in his neck like cords as
he lifted the tree. The muscles in his thighs strained
against his trousers. But those were the only indications
of the mighty nature of the task.

'I hope he doesn't hurt himself,' said Ellie.

But the tree had moved, and Charlie was smiling.
'We can do it,' she heard him say.

They did. Foot by foot the three men heaved and
grunted, half lifting, half shoving the tree round to the
point where it no longer blocked the roadway.

'Thanks, mate,' said Tony, panting. 'We'll have that
cup of tea now. JB and I'll cut it up into pieces and
take it back to the station for firewood.'

'They'd better be small pieces,' said JB. 'Unless
you're going to get Charlie back again.'

'Come on, JB!' growled Tony. 'We can do it. We've
got to be half as strong as he is.'

'Speak for yourself,' said JB. 'I'm damn sure I'm not.'

Back at the ranger station, Ellie sipped her tea
thoughtfully. Till now she had thought of Charlie as a
good-natured, harmless sort of chap. She had seen him
now as something else again — as a man so immensely
powerful that he could probably pick most other men
up and hurl them through the wall. It occurred to Ellie
that it was a good thing he did have a placid nature. An
aggressive man of Charlie's strength would be dangerous to be near. She wondered if he *was* ever angry, and
concluded that she was not anxious to see it.

Once again, as they demolished the last of Marje's
cake, Ellie found herself in observation of Marian and
Charlie, and now Tony.

She could see no symptoms of love for Marian in the
senior ranger. At times he seemed to speak to her with
a sort of brusque fondness, but there was nothing

lover-like in his dark countenance at all. Perhaps one day soon Marian would get sick of waiting for Tony to notice her and turn her attention elsewhere.

And how much further need she look than Charlie, who, with his good-natured kindness, would be an excellent match for her? Ellie was puzzled to find that she didn't feel as happy as she ought to at the thought. But she didn't have time to dwell on it. It was time for the rangers to go and check the picnic ground for trash and smouldering fires.

The rangers accompanied them out to the car. Ellie said goodbye to them, promising to come again, and saw Charlie give Marian not only his friendly hug, but also a brief kiss. The smile that passed between them was intimate and warm. Ellie felt once again that odd little twinge of disquiet.

'Will you come again?' Charlie asked as they drove away.

'Yes. I like them a lot. And I love the park.'

'Marian likes you,' he said warmly. 'She's comfortable with you. It's nice to see you get on so well with her.'

'I think she's an awfully nice person,' Ellie replied truthfully.

Charlie's voice was full of unmistakable affection as he answered, 'She is. None better.' There was a note of regret as he added, 'Things aren't easy for her. She's not always valued as she ought to be. But perhaps that will change.'

Ellie caught the note of sadness, and thought, He does care. They were silent after that till they reached the turn-off to the Barr's peak look-out.

'Have you been to the look-out?' Charlie asked, and when Ellie said no swung the car off the main road into the parking area. 'It's worth it,' he said. 'Only a minute's walk.'

He was right. The look-out was a rocky sandstone clifftop that gave out over the bushland and the undulating plains all the way to the coast. Ellie stepped up on to a sandstone shelf and peered over the edge. The face fell away sheer. She felt Charlie's hand on her waist. 'Don't go over,' came his deep voice beside her.

She stepped back a little, but stayed on the shelf, so that she was almost as tall as he was. From there, she looked around. The sun was setting, the shadows dark in the gorge. To the west, the horizon was deep orange, fading into purple sky above, with a few silver stars. It was breathtaking. 'It's lovely,' she whispered.

He made a little noise of assent, and they stood touching, silently sharing it, till Ellie said, 'I don't think I ever want to see another city,' and he answered,

'No. You *do* like the bush, don't you?'

'I love everything about it!' she said. 'The landscape, the trees, the animals, the friendliness, the caring. Even — the need for self-reliance.' She turned a little to face him. 'Do you understand?'

The dying sun fell on Charlie's face, on a level with her own. He was smiling. 'Yes, I understand,' he said, his eyes warm on her. She could hear that he really did, and smiled back with the pleasure of it.

Then his smile faded, as did her own, and there was a frozen moment of locked eyes, clear grey and green, before Charlie moved towards her. And his mouth met Ellie's — gently, agonisingly gently, then more vehemently, searching for a response.

She was powerlesss to withhold it. The sensation was overwhelming. It was wonderful — more wonderful than anything she had dreamed possible. His lips moved against hers in a slow, compelling exploration that sent a surge of fire through her. Her heart burst into a crazy gallop, and her breath came quickly, her chest tight with desire.

She stood still, unresisting, aware that his breath was as fast as hers. He moved his mouth, her soft lips gliding under it, and it drew from her a tiny strangled sound, almost a moan. At that he jerked his head back, his eyes searching hers, and in his face there dawned a look of pain. She saw him swallow, and take a ragged breath, then he stepped back with a hasty movement, saying hoarsely, 'I'm sorry! I'm sorry. I shouldn't have done that.'

Ellie found she couldn't speak. She was still reeling from the shock of it, and the sensations it had aroused in her.

He shook his head, as though to clear his vision, and drew another deep breath. 'I shouldn't have done that,' he repeated. 'Forgive me, Ellie.' Then he made a helpless gesture, and turned to walk away.

Ellie found her legs shaking, and sat down suddenly on the rock. She stared ahead of her, trying desperately to gather her wits. But the only thought that her brain would form was a question: why?

Then, as her breathing slowed, and her brain came to order, she realised there were any number of whys. Why had he done it? Why did she repond to him like that? And why was he so appalled at what he had done? She didn't have answers for any of them. She could only sit and wait till her limbs ceased to quake.

And then she heard his footfall, and he had returned to sit beside her. He sat forward, with his elbows on his knees, rubbing his face with both hands. At last he moved back, letting out a long breath, and gently took her hand. 'Poor Ellie,' he said in a low, rueful voice. 'What an oaf I am! I didn't mean to do that. I won't do it again.'

Ellie forced herself to look at him, and saw the regret in his face. She gave her head a little shake, and tried to give a smile. 'It's all right, Charlie,' she said, her voice little more than a whisper. She wanted to add, I didn't mind, even perhaps, I loved it! but he so clearly did mind, so clearly regretted it, that it was impossible to say.

His hand tightened around hers. 'Kind Ellie,' he said. 'Forgive me. Don't fear that it will happen again.'

He sounded so concerned that she found she wanted to comfort him. She gave his hand a squeeze in reply, and managed to say in a much more normal tone, 'Don't worry, Charlie. It really is all right. I understand.'

But as they walked back to the car she reflected that that was a lie. She didn't understand anything. On the drive back to the Base, she grappled with it in her mind. And it wasn't long before she came to the conclusion that Simon had been wrong. Charlie did know women were different. He was a perfect biological specimen who responded to them exactly as he should. Close to her, at the end of a day spent with Marian, he'd reacted with the arousal that proclaimed him to be as virile as he looked. But he was a man, not an animal, and she was the wrong woman. It was Marian he wanted. It was the only explanation that would fit.

And that, Ellie knew, left her with a little problem. Whatever her feelings for him on a higher plane, whatever her reservations about his softness, there was no question that Charlie Carmody turned her on. In future she would have to keep her distance, before it became embarrassingly obvious to him. If it wasn't now. On that topic she was undecided. Perhaps he'd been too involved with his own emotions to notice hers. She could only pray that it was so.

CHAPTER SEVEN

BACK at the Base, Ellie heard Simon's car draw up below, and decided she wouldn't go down to the common-room before dinner after all. After yesterday, she had no wish to encounter Simon again before she had to. Only Charlie and Paul were in the common-room by the fire.

Paul gave him a sardonic glance. 'So — we wondered whether you had got lost somewhere, Simon.'

Not at all,' he replied. 'I know the way to Bega very well.'

Paul raised one eyebrow. 'Oh. Are you still welcome there, Simon, after all this time?'

Simon grinned. 'It took a bit of charm,' he admitted.

'But of course,' Paul said. 'Of charm, you have enough.'

'How kind,' Simon murmured.

'But — what about decency, Simon? One is not blind. One has seen you with Ellie. Do you mean to break Ellie's heart?'

Simon opened his mouth as though to speak, then shut it again. Then, finally, with a studied nonchalance, he said, 'I'm not responsible for Ellie's heart. She'll have to look after it herself.' And with that he hauled himself from the chair and walked away.

Paul watched him go with narrowed eyes. 'Really, one wishes that young man would just once meet with a defeat, eh, Charlie?'

Charlie, lounging in another armchair, returned

Paul's look with eyes that were unusually hard. 'Perhaps he will,' was his reply.

Paul made a hopeless gesture. 'Ellie is so warm, so loving. If one could tell her what he is without hurting her. . .'

'Don't try,' said Charlie bluntly. 'You'll only do harm. Besides. . .'

'Besides what?' Paul asked.

'It doesn't matter,' said Charlie, but he stayed where he was for a long itme, staring into the fire as though deep in thought.

'Ellie!' Simon's voice made her jump. She thought he must have been waiting for her to come downstairs to dinner. Instinctively she drew back, only to find that Simon had gone down on one knee on the carpet.

'I abase myself! I humble myself! I beg your forgiveness,' he cried theatrically. 'Kick me! I deserve it.' With this he peered up through his lashes with a look of supplication which drew a smile from her despite herself.

'Oh, get up, Simon!' she said in an exasperated tone.

'No. Not until you've kicked me,' he vowed. 'I won't feel better till then.'

Ellie gave a choke of laughter. 'You'd better get up before I do!' she declared. 'Of all the rotten things to have said. . .'

He did rise, and his face seemed sincerely contrite. 'I know,' he said. 'I've been torturing myself with the memory of it for two days.'

This Ellie very much doubted. But she forbore to say so, and only said instead, 'Well, it doesn't matter. Thank you for apologising. Let's be friends, shall we?'

He smiled. 'Thank you. It's better than I deserve.'

'Probably,' she said, and grinned.

Simon grinned back. 'I do like you,' he said softly. 'You're like no one else.'

Ellie was glad to make peace. They had to live and work together, and she'd been more than half afraid that he'd come back from wherever he'd gone in the same ugly mood as he'd left. But he was cheerful and pleasant over dinner, passing her things and exerting himself to entertain her, so she did forgive him, and treated him as she'd done before.

If Paul and Charlie were rather more quiet than usual, and if they didn't appear so pleased at the reconciliation, Ellie didn't notice, and Simon didn't care.

'Good. Now the third roll,' Charlie said softly in her ear. Ellie was doing a plaster. Mostly the houseman did them, but it was useful if the sisters could do them too. Young Amanda, who had fallen off her horse and broken her radius, didn't mind who did it as long as they agreed to autograph it at the end. Charlie Carmody was helping Ellie, sitting at her side and holding the arm.

'That's it. Nice and smooth, so there won't be any bumps to stick into her and make it uncomfortable.'

'I'm sorry I'm splashing you,' said Ellie. 'I'm beginning to realise why you doctors make such a mess when you do this. I'll never criticise you again!' She made a comical face of dismay at him, but he only smiled down into her eyes.

'You're doing very well,' he said encouragingly. 'Not making half as much mess as I do. OK, now we smooth it. Like this——' Charlie took her hand and rubbed it over the plaster so that she was smoothing it with the heel of her hand. 'Lightly like that,' he said.

The end result wasn't too bad. The arm and hand

were in the correct anatomical position for healing, and the plaster was moulded adequately to the shape of the arm.

'Will you sign it now?' asked Amanda, but Charlie shook his head.

'Not yet. We have to allow it a few minutes to dry, or the ink will run.' He continued to sit, supporting Amanda's forearm under his.

Ellie had been feeling flustered ever since he'd come to sit so close beside her that she could feel her own leg warm against his long, muscled thigh. It wasn't proving to be easy to keep her distance from Charlie Carmody, she reflected drily. For the last week, since she'd made that resolution, she had seen more of him than ever. Whenever she turned around, he seemed to be there, looking down out of smiling grey eyes. The close contact now assured her that her earlier feelings hadn't been a fluke. She found him physically exciting. It disturbed her. She didn't understand it. She wished he would go away, and wanted him to stay.

'That should do. You can feel the heat coming from it now as the plaster sets. Sister can sign it now.'

Charlie bent over her and watched as she signed her name with a flourish with a felt-tipped pen, adding a sweet little daisy at one side.

Amanda laughed. 'That's lovely! Now you, Dr Charlie!' she commanded.

Charlie took the pen from Ellie's hand, scrawled his name, then drew a heart with an arrow through it. Inside he put 'A.L. loves horses' — A.L. being Amanda's initials — which was an even bigger hit.

'Draw another one, Dr Charlie!' said Amanda. 'Put who you love!' But Charlie laughingly shook his head. 'Why not?' she cried.

'It's a secret,' he said.

'Why?' she asked with ten-year-old directness.

Charlie hesitated, then said, 'I haven't told her yet.'

'Why?' Amanda pursued.

Again there was a pause, then, 'It's not the right time,' he said.

Ellie was sure he must have been grateful when Amanda turned to her. 'You write yours, Ellie!'

Ellie had already thought. She took the pen and drew a heart, and the others watched silently as she wrote 'E.S. loves Hercules'.

Charlie gave a shout of laughter, and Amanda said, 'Who's he?'

But Ellie only got to her feet, laughing, and said, 'Oh, a very handsome chap!' She went to get a sling, thinking of Charlie. He was right. It wasn't the right time. Marian wasn't ready for him yet.

'Are you going to the mess dinner?' asked Caroline again at lunchtime, and Ellie nodded.

'I thought I'd like to. Are you?'

'Yes, we always go. Is it permitted to ask whether you *are* going with Simon?' Caroline enquired drily.

Ellie smiled. 'It's permitted, but I'm not. I've decided to go by myself. Or rather, with Barbara Knox. She's going alone, too.'

'Uh-huh,' said Caroline, and looked at her quizzically. 'The plot thickens,' she said.

Ellie laughed. 'Honestly, Caroline—there's no plot.'

Caroline only grinned.

Ellie had been to hospital mess dinners before. They were formal affairs, with a sit-down meal, an after-dinner speaker and dancing. She was glad she'd brought the right kind of dress. It was sea-green, just below knee-length, hugging her form to the hips, then ending in a graceful flare.

'Wow!' said Barbara when she saw it. 'You'll put us country girls to shame! You look like you stepped out of *Vogue*!'

'Thank you!' said Ellie, smiling shyly. 'You look nice too!'

'OK!' said Barbara. 'Let's go and knock 'em dead!'

They had taken their dresses with them to Bega, and changed in the room of one of the Bega nurses, Barbara's friend. It meant they could sail down to the hospital dining-room uncrushed, and rather early as well. The room had been well and truly rearranged for the event, with set tables up one end and an area for dancing at the other. There were a few people there, all of them from Bega, but Barbara knew them, so it wasn't long before they both had a drink and company.

Simon was the first of the Base crowd to arrive, and didn't take long to come to Ellie's side. 'You look ravishing!' he said, in a tone that Ellie almost thought sincere, then added, 'How clever of you to choose a dress that matches your eyes.'

There was a fierce glint in his that made Ellie feel uncomfortable. She was glad when Paul appeared, and came to stand at her side.

'Did you drive?' she asked Paul, for something to say.

'But yes!' he answered. 'Me, I will not willingly drive with Charlie. He is too slow!'

'Oh, did you drive Charlie?'

'No, no. He comes. Some time he comes.'

And he did come, not too long after. Ellie turned and saw him standing a little distance away, and felt a little shock run through her.

She had given no thought to how Charlie would look in formal wear. She had never seen him in anything but comfortable work clothes, bush clobber or theatre pyjamas. He didn't give the impression of a man who wasted time considering his appearance. Her overall image of Charlie was of a man dedicated to comfort and practicality.

He looked magnificent. He stood with the stem of a wine glass between his long fingers, tall, broad-shouldered and immaculate in a dinner-suit and a snowy white dress-shirt and white tie. For a moment, Ellie stared. Her imprisoned gaze took in the excellent cut of a coat that seemed moulded to his form and the general impression of elegant neatness. His shoes were impeccably shined; there was not a hair out of place. The dark dress clothes perfectly suited him. Ellie realised that this handsome stranger would have drawn her gaze had she met him anywhere.

He seemed to sense her scrutiny, and turned in her direction. The grey eyes caught hers and he smiled, and Ellie felt a swift contraction in the region of her stomach. Before she'd had time to recover, he was at her side, smiling down at her.

Ellie willed herself to smile back, a normal social smile. 'You look wonderful, Charlie,' she said, trying not to sound surprised.

Charlie might have been embarrassed at the compliment, or might not. He said nothing, merely surveying her for a moment, his eyes coming to rest after his inspection on her face. 'So do you,' he said softly at last.

It had been oddly disconcerting, as disconcerting as the unfamiliar light lurking in his eyes. Everything made her feel as though she didn't know him — that here was a new Charlie standing at her side. Again, she felt that swift contraction, and realised that this Charlie turned her on more than ever.

They were seated on opposite sides of the table at

dinner, Charlie separated from Simon by a female
house surgeon from Bega. The seating gave Ellie the
opportunity to compare the two men, and Ellie wondered suddenly why she had thought Simon the better-
looking of the two. For Simon's prettiness couldn't
compare with Charlie's manly handsomeness. She studied his face anew—the clear brow, the strong, even
features, the fine, light eyes and that eminently kissable
mouth. Ellie found that her heart was speeding, and
wondered for a moment what kind of madness this
was. She wasn't in love with Charlie. He wasn't her
type. He was too yielding. And yet, though she tried
to keep her eyes away, they would keep straying back.

He caught her at it once, and gave another slow-
curving smile. After that, Ellie devoted herself to her
neighbours, and was glad when dinner was over and
she could turn her attention to the speaker of the night.

But when that was done and the music started, things
became even more alarming. Ellie's heart plunged as
she felt Charlie's hand on her arm. 'Are you brave
enough to take a risk with me?' he asked.

Paul Vassy had seen Charlie beat Simon to it. '*Eh
bien*, consider what you are doing, Ellie,' Paul joked.
'With Charlie's weight, he could break all the bones in
your feet.'

Ellie gave a strained little laugh. She wasn't sure she
should dance with him. For a moment she thought of
refusing, but then somehow found herself on her feet.
She let him take her hand and hoped it wasn't trembling as he led her on to the floor.

Paul had defamed him. In fact he danced very well,
with the ease and grace of a natural athlete. Ellie was
surprised for a moment, then, remembering his relaxed
stride as he'd walked through the bush in the park,
concluded that she might have known.

He held her lightly at first in the circle of his arm, their bodies barely touching. But, even so, she was close enough to the warmth of him, and to catch his masculine scent. And it was as she had thought it would be—pleasurable and exciting.

She felt the gently pressure of his hand on her back as he steered her away from another couple, and it was Ellie, not Charlie, who stumbled against his foot.

She glanced up. 'I'm sorry,' she said.

He was looking down at her, his eyes warm, that slow smile on his mouth. Tonight, she found it arousing. She felt his hand tighten on hers and he drew her closer against him.

It was certainly harder to lose one's step that way. Their two bodies moved as one. His arm pressed her against the length of him. She felt his supple movements and the latent power in them, and felt every nerve in her body tauten. It was hard to breathe. An agonising fire flared up in her and seemed to sear her wherever their bodies touched.

He laid her hand against his chest and covered it with his own, and Ellie knew from some instinct that he was looking down. Against her will she glanced up at him, and encountered his eyes, dark tonight, and in their depths that light she had seen before. Something clutched at her, some place vital, and her heart lurched into an even faster beat. The corners of his mouth turned up, just faintly, and Ellie suddenly felt he knew. The hand on her back stirred and pressed her against him harder, its movement surely a caress!

Ellie's mind whirled. If she hadn't known better, she would have said that Charlie was making a move on her! But that couldn't be! And she didn't want it. She was physically attracted to him—powerfully so. But that was all it was. And yet she felt herself melt against him, so that her cheek was cradled against his shoulder; and she felt his hand move again sensually across her back, so that she was almost completely enfolded by his arm.

Ellie existed in a dream-like state for the rest of the dance. Then the music stopped, but Charlie still held her for a moment. Then slowly he let her go, his hand grazing across her back as she moved away.

She met his eyes with difficulty. But his were smiling.

'Thank you,' he said, and retired as Simon came to take his place.

It was a relief at first to dance with Simon. Her pulse-rate returned to normal and she was able to breathe freely again. Once more she became aware of her surroundings. With Charlie she had been lost to everything, even the spectacle of Simon flirting out-rageously with the young female doctor from Bega, which no one else in the room, including Charlie, had been able to miss.

But the relief was short-lived, and came to an end when she realised that Simon was determined to dance more intimately than even Charlie had done. 'Don't, Simon!' she said, pulling away from an embrace that would have been too close to be comfortable even if she had liked it. 'I can't dance like that.'

'You seemed to manage it with Charlie!' he said, and Ellie could hear the anger in his voice.

Oh, no! she thought. Don't pick a fight with me here. Really, Simon wearied her. She wished he would find someone else to think about. But she said nothing more, and even gritted her teeth when he stroked her back seductively, in the interests of avoiding a public quarrel. But when his hand moved down to touch her buttock, she'd had enough.

She thrust him back from her, and said hotly, 'Don't,

Simon! You are really making me angry. I don't want that!'

Ellie saw his eyes flash and his face whiten. The small mouth, which had looked merely petulant before, drew into a tight, angry line. 'What *do* you want, Ellie?' he flung at her.

'I don't want anything!' she said.

'I don't believe you! I know what you want, what you need. You're just afraid of it. Afraid of me.' Simon made an effort to master himself, and managed a gentler tone. 'What is it, Ellie? Those cracks about other women? You don't have to worry about that. You're different. If I had you, I wouldn't want anyone else.'

Ellie almost felt sorry for him. It still hadn't occurred to him that she just might not be interested. She didn't know what to say. 'Simon, it's not that,' she said softly. 'It's just that we really don't like the same things. It just wouldn't work for me.'

'You won't give it a chance!' he said vehemently, all his anger rekindled.

Ellie thought he sounded like a six-year-old, but her own temper was starting to rise. Really, she might be spared this on the dance-floor! 'It doesn't have a chance, Simon!' she snapped.

'Why don't you be honest with yourself?' he raged.

'Why don't you shut up?' she cried, goaded beyond endurance.

'Don't tell me to shut up!' He was almost shouting.

'I don't have to put up with this!' And with that Ellie jerked herself from his grasp. Oblivious to curious eyes, she turned on her heel and walked off without looking back.

If she had, she would have seen on his face a look of fury that might have made her afraid.

Ellie splashed her face with water in the bathroom, then patched up her make-up. She sighed. How ridiculous. And how embarrassing. Why couldn't he get it into his head? Perhaps she should have been brutally honest. She could have said, Simon, at first I was flattered by you. Then bored. And now I really find you rather repulsive. But she couldn't imagine being as cruel as that. She screwed up her courage to go back to the dining-room, and behave as though nothing had happened at all. She wondered how soon Barbara might be persuaded to go home.

CHAPTER EIGHT

BACK in the dining-room, Ellie behaved as though the questioning glances didn't exist. She made her way back to the table, spying Barbara's figure on the dance-floor. Barbara didn't look as though she'd be in any hurry to leave. Ellie became aware that Charlie had risen and pulled out the vacated chair next to his. 'Sit here,' he said and she did as she was bid. He seated himself again, and introduced her to the people he was talking to. One was the med super of Bega, another an anaesthetist like Charlie, and the third the sister in charge of theatres. They had enough in common for conversation to thrive, and Ellie soon felt much more comfortable, and no longer wished to go home.

She even began to enjoy herself. They seemed like nice people, outgoing and easy. She found herself joining in less self-consciously than she would have thought possible, even making them laugh. Sitting there among pleasant company with Charlie smiling down at her now and then, his arm thrown along the back of her chair, she forgot the existence of Simon, though she was facing the part of the room where he was. If Charlie's eyes sometimes strayed to him and discerned the fact that he was behaving scandalously with the female doctor, he gave no sign of it.

When their little group showed signs of breaking up, he invited her once again to dance. With a little apprehension, she put up her arms to him, but this time he held her lightly, a little distance away. She was conscious of an irrational feeling of disappointment,

95

and cursed herself for it. She knew she ought to be relieved.

And yet, as the dance went on, she realised that this was more tantalising than dancing closely. From time to time she brushed against him, touching his body with her hip or a breast. Each time she felt a sweet tension seize her, and wanted to press herself further into his arms. But to do so was alien to Ellie. She wasn't made that way.

She realised all at once that he was studying her face, and started a little, wondering what he had read in it. 'Shall I drive you home?' he asked.

At first she thought it was a sexual invitation, but then she saw his eyes stray to Simon, and she realised what it was. Charlie had assumed that she had come with Simon. He had seen their disagreement, and what Simon was doing now. It was a rescue that he offered, nothing else.

Ellie opened her mouth to say she'd come with Barbara, and then found she'd changed her mind. It would be nice to drive back with Charlie. She wanted to, and Barbara wouldn't mind at all. So she simply said. 'Yes. Thank you.'

'Tell me when you'd like to go,' he said.

Ellie shook her head. 'Whenever you would.'

Charlie smiled. 'I don't mind. Any time. Are you tired?'

'A little,' she admitted. 'I don't mind going any time you want.'

'Shall we go at the end of this, then?' he suggested, and Ellie nodded. She really had had enough. This slow, enticing dance was taking its toll on her. She was glad when the music stopped.

'I'll join you outside, shall I?' Ellie asked and he

GET 4 BOOKS
A CUDDLY TEDDY
AND A MYSTERY GIFT

Return this card, and we'll send you 4 Mills & Boon romances, absolutely FREE! We'll even pay the postage and packing for you!

We're making you this offer to introduce to you the benefits of Mills & Boon Reader Service: FREE home delivery of brand-new Mills & Boon romances, at least a month before they're available in the shops, FREE gifts and a monthly Newsletter packed with special offers and information.

Accepting these FREE books places you under no obligation to buy, you may cancel at any time, even after receiving just your free shipment.

Yes, please send me 4 free Mills & Boon romances, a cuddly teddy and a mystery gift as explained above. Please also reserve a Reader Service subscription for me. If I decide to subscribe, I shall receive 6 superb new titles every month for just £11.40 postage and packing free. If I decide not to subscribe I shall write to you within 10 days. The free books and gifts will be mine to keep in any case. I understand that I am under no obligation whatsoever. I may cancel or suspend my subscription at any time simply by writing to you.

Ms/Mrs/Miss/Mr _____ 10A4R

Address _____

_____

_____ Postcode _____

Signature _____
I am over 18 years of age.

Get 4 books a cuddly teddy and mystery gift FREE!

SEE BACK OF CARD FOR DETAILS

Mills & Boon Reader Service,
FREEPOST
P.O. Box 236
Croydon
CR9 9EL

No stamp needed

nodded and went. Ellie quickly found Barbara and told her she was tired. Charlie had offered to take her back.

'Oh, that's good!' said Barbara. 'I'd really rather stay a while. I'll bring your things.'

Ellie thanked her, and went to collect her bag.

'Liz Hale's an interesting person. She paints. Water-colour landscapes. Very good.' Charlie's voice was companionable in the darkness of the moving car.

'Oh, does she? How clever!' He was talking of the sister they'd been sitting with. 'You really know every-thing about people, living in the country, don't you?'

'Well, not everything.' Charlie's voice held amuse-ment. 'But quite a lot. We're really part of a com-munity, even if it's rather far flung.'

'Yes. You know all the farmers in the district, don't you?'

'Mmm,' Charlie agreed. 'They come to Cas often enough. But I know them from the bushfire organis-ation, too.'

'Oh. Are you in that?'

'Yes. The hospital should function as part of the wider community. Not hold itself aloof. I like to take part in things that concern us all.'

'Have there been any fires?' Ellie asked.

'Every year. In summer, but also in the driest part of winter. Those are usually caused by careless humans. In summer they can be set off by the sun shining on a piece of glass on the ground.'

'Also left by careless humans,' Ellie said, and Charlie agreed.

They talked companionably all the way back to Berringar. It was strange how she and Charlie found so much to say.

'Do you like dancing?' he asked when they were almost there. 'You do it well.'

'Yes. Thank you,' she said, and added shyly, 'So do you.'

Then they were silent as Charlie drove through the hospital gates, Ellie thinking once more of their dance. And as she remembered it she felt again that current of excitement, that tightness in her chest.

He parked the car and opened the door for her, giving her his hand. Then they walked inside together, into the darkened quarters, with only a lamp in the entrance hall showing them where to go. There Ellie stopped and turned to him, intending to thank him and say goodnight. But he suddenly reached out a hand and took hers, and said quietly, 'Come.'

Ellie's heart gave a lunge, and the blood rushed to her face. What did he mean? But already he was showing her, leading her into the common-room, which was lit only by the glow of the dying fire. He drew her by the hand to the sofa before it, and let her go, removed his coat and threw it on a chair, then crouched to put more wood on the fire and stoke it up.

Ellie's mind was racing. Her mouth was dry. She sat down automatically, thinking, What does he want?

Then, when the fire blazed, he came back to her, and sat down by her side. He pulled at his bow-tie to untie it, and undid the top button of his shirt. She saw his face in the firelight — composed, half smiling, his eyes warm.

'Ellie,' he said softly, and took her by the shoulders. Then slowly, ever so slowly, he brought his lips to hers and kissed her tenderly and long. Finally he moved back from her, and looked into her eyes. He was silent for a moment. He might have been waiting for his breathing, which was a little rapid, to slow. Then he said in the same soft, low voice, 'I know I said I wouldn't do that again. But I'm a little slow.' His eyes warmed with a smile. 'It wasn't till later that it struck me that you liked it.'

Ellie stared up into his face, unable to make a reply. But he didn't give her a chance to anyway. Charlie kissed her again. His big arms went round her and pulled her lightly against his chest. His mouth moved on hers with a tantalising gentleness that made her long for more. Ellie thought dimly that it was meant to, that Charlie knew exactly what he was about. But if she'd wanted to withold her response, she couldn't have. In a few short moments, Ellie was aflame. She abandoned any attempt at thinking, and simply pressed her own lips harder against his.

And then she felt his arms tighten, and his lips move more insistently on hers. Her breasts were pressed against him, her heart hammering like a machine. He lifted his lips from her several times, and gave her fierce, short kisses that made her gasp. Then, when her arms went involuntarily round him, he lay back and pulled her down on top of him.

Ellie knew a moment of misgiving, but almost as soon as it started he had kissed it away. She felt him lift her so that he could put his feet up, and she lay full-length on top of him, and realised he was just as aroused as she. The alarm returned, but he didn't give her time to think about it. He kissed her fiercely again till she was panting and could only kiss him back. Only then did he roll her a little to one side, and with gentle fingers trace the curve of her breast. She opened her mouth to utter a protest, but, with his eyes on hers, he drew one finger over its hardened peak, and it came out as a moan. He kissed her again then, and continued to stroke her, and Ellie suddenly knew she was being made love to by an expert, and she would do anything he liked. The desire seemed to fill her to bursting, and a delicious sense of tension invaded her belly and loins. She could feel his straining hardness, and the slam of his heart against his ribs. She longed for him to invade her, to take her to him here and now.

Ellie rolled herself suddenly back on top of him, wanting to be as close to him as she could, and the full weight of her body on him made him give a groan. Ellie lay still, and heard him struggle for breath.

'Did I hurt you?' she whispered urgently.

And he said, 'No!' in a hoarse voice. 'Only—I wasn't expecting that.' And she heard a note of humour as he added, 'You've thrown my calculations out.'

She raised her head, puzzled, and he said, 'Stay still, Ellie! Just for a bit.' She saw that he was smiling, but his pupils were enormous, and there was a look of fire in his eyes. She knew all at once that he was afraid of losing control. His chest rose and fell rapidly under hers, and when he reached up to stroke her face his fingers trembled. He closed his eyes for an instant, as though in pain, then gave her a rueful smile.

'You'll have to roll off me,' he said gently, and she did what he asked, sitting on the edge of the sofa by his legs. He lay still for a minute, then sat up and swung his legs down, gathering her to his chest. She felt him give a little sigh.

They sat there like that for a while, then Ellie moved back from him and looked up with troubled eyes. 'Charlie,' she whispered, 'I don't understand.'

He looked back at her with his calm half-smile, the grey eyes warm in the firelight. Gently, he stroked her flushed cheek with his hand. 'What don't you understand?' he asked.

'Why we did that. Why *I* did that.'

Charlie didn't answer for a moment. He might have been thinking. Then he said softly, 'It was nice, hmm?'

Ellie nodded, and dropped her eyes, but he put his hand under her chin and forced it up. There was a little frown in his eyes. 'Don't be ashamed,' he said.

She brought her eyes back to meet his squarely, and said, 'Charlie, we can't always do what's nice just — just because it is!'

'Does there have to be another reason?' he asked slowly.

'Yes. Yes, I think so. Things like this. M-making love. . .' Her voice trailed away shyly.

Charlie pulled her closer against him, and turned so that they faced the fire. He rested his cheek lightly on the top of her head. 'Why?' he asked.

'Because — otherwise — it's cheap and — ' But he didn't let her finish. He gripped her hard, and his voice was more fervent than she'd ever heard it.

'It wasn't. And it isn't. It could never be that between you and me.'

And somehow Ellie knew he was right, even though they weren't in love. There was too much respect between them for it ever to be cheap. 'I'm sorry, Charlie. I'm sorry,' she said. 'You're right.'

She felt him relax. 'So why?' he said, and dropped a kiss on her hair.

She gave a short little laugh. 'I don't know. Convention, I suppose. The — the convention is you're supposed to be in love.'

Ellie had the feeling that Charlie was restraining himself from making a reply. She hoped suddenly that he didn't think she wanted him to say he loved her. She didn't want him to lie. But perhaps he was only thinking. For presently he said, 'Don't think too much, Ellie. Trust what you feel. If it feels right to you, it will be. Do you understand?' He moved her back to look at her face.

'Foggily,' she said, and gave a little grin.

He gave a sudden rumble of laughter, and grinned down at her, looking quite like the Charlie of every day. Her eyes swept over his beautiful, good-natured face, and travelled down to the powerful neck, with the shirt open on it and the tie hanging loose about it. And all at once she was no longer sure that she *didn't* love Charlie. She knew that she wanted to kiss him again.

And she knew that he knew it. She saw the corners of his mouth lift, and he said softly, 'Trust your feelings.'

Ellie returned his smile with a small shy one of her own, then slowly leaned towards him and kissed him on the neck once, twice. She felt him draw a deeper breath, but he didn't move. She brought her face up to his and saw once again the burning light in his eyes, but still he did nothing, until she had put her lips to his. Then he enfolded her and kissed her as fiercely as he had before. At the end of the kiss a cry broke from her. 'Charlie! Charlie, I'm afraid! I don't know why!'

Then he cradled her gently, stroking her and saying, 'Don't be. There's nothing to fear.' And finally he sat her upright, and gave another sigh. 'Go to bed now,' he said. 'You're tired. Go to bed, and don't think any more.'

Ellie did, and, contrary to her expectation, fell asleep straight away.

Ellie woke to a crisp Sunday with frost on her window, but the sun already shining outside. She snuggled down further under the covers, full of that delicious Sunday feeling, glad that she didn't have to get up. This was just what she needed — to lie here and think.

Weeks ago she had thought she knew Charlie Carmody. But with each new revelation of his character she felt she knew him less. The Charlie of last night had surprised her the most. Nothing had prepared her for the stylish stranger who had begun to practise his expert seduction on her from the first moment of their meeting at the dinner. For now she was sure that was how it had been.

To what end she wasn't sure. In the cold light of day she could see that he hadn't intended to make love to her in earnest on the common-room sofa, with the likelihood that others would soon come home. Perhaps he'd been intending to adjourn elsewhere, or perhaps it had been merely round one. Charlie, she knew, was a patient man.

And a practical man. He didn't have Ellie's scruples. He didn't need to be in love to enjoy a physical attraction, any more than his possums did. It didn't even matter that he was fond of someone else.

Ellie frowned. Was he? She might have imagined that. And all at once she knew that she was hoping she had. The thought had never pleased her. She suddenly knew that though she was not in love with Charlie Carmody she was perilously close. Only that small doubt about his character, a suspicion that he was too yielding, kept her back. But she had better be careful, anyway. Charlie hadn't said that he loved her. It had better not happen again.

She rose eventually, and put on some jeans and a warm woolly jumper. When she went downstairs, her heart gave a thump to see that Charlie was the only one there. He was sitting in an armchair by the window, surrounded by the papers. He looked up when she came in.

'A med super's work is never done,' she said lightly, trying for poise.

Charlie smiled, and said quietly, 'Come here,' and Ellie's heart promptly turned over in her chest. But when she did he only took her hand and said, 'Did you sleep well?'

'Like a corpse,' she said, and he grinned.

'If you want to see someone corpse-like, Sister Knox is in the dining-room downing Alka-Seltzer and aspirin.'

Ellie gave a ripple of laughter. 'Oh, no! Poor Barb!'

'She's paying for her sins,' he said, and then his eyes scanned Ellie's face. 'Not paying for ours this morning, Ellie?' he asked gently, and she felt herself colour up. But she managed to smile and to shake her head.

'No.'

'Good,' he said, and released her hand.

Ellie, as she went into the dining-room, was conscious of a feeling of disappointment. When she had just vowed to steer clear of involvement with Charlie, it was irrational to wish he'd said and done more. But so it was.

'Oh, Barb!' Her friend did look somewhat the worse for wear.

'Don't say it. I know it was my own fault,' said Barbara, grinning feebly. 'You look disgusting, Ellie. Healthy.'

'Well, I went home early. Remember?'

'Vaguely,' said her friend. 'Oh, yes. With Charlie. Behave himself, did he?'

'What do you think?' asked Ellie lightly.

'Don't ask me to think!' groaned Barbara. 'Wouldn't have blamed him, though, if he didn't. You did look beautiful, Ellie.'

'Thank you,' Ellie said shyly.

Barbara sipped her tea. 'I wonder about Charlie. All that virile maleness going to waste. If he's ever shared it with the nursing staff, I haven't heard about it. There was a rumour once about an ICU sister we had. But she was as close as an oyster. You couldn't tell. He couldn't be a virgin, though, with a body and face like his.'

Ellie was damned sure he wasn't, but she wasn't going to say so.

'Nothing?' asked Barbara. 'Not even a goodnight kiss?'

Ellie thought swiftly. Sometimes the truth was the best lie. 'He ravished me on the sofa,' she said.

Barbara laughed, as Ellie had known she would, and only said jokingly, 'Half your luck!'

Ellie spent the day quietly, reading and doing little chores. Charlie worked all the morning in the common-room with his customary absorption, not seeming to know she was there. In the afternoon, he disappeared in the direction of the wards, and Ellie knew a feeling of chagrin. Was he just going to ignore her now? But she knew it was stupid. It was what she wanted, after all.

In the late afternoon, he returned to a room that had filled up with other people. Paul and Simon were there, and Alison and Pete. Charlie sat down and had tea with them, listening to their talk and occasionally offering a remark. But he didn't speak to Ellie any more than to the rest, nor did his eyes seek hers as hers sought him. And the little feeling of disappointment grew into a definite feeling of pain. It hadn't meant anything to him. She had looked attractive, and he had been hungry for physical contact.

Then, just as she had decided that she was glad, and

that that was one problem behind her, he rose to his feet and stopped beside her chair. 'Come and have a look at the possums,' he invited and Ellie found herself obediently getting to her feet and following him outside.

He crouched by the enclosure and Ellie took her old seat, to see that a change had taken place. Hercules was showing a definite interest in Jez, and Casanova didn't like it at all. Ellie saw him take a nip at Hercules, who turned and dealt with it summarily, with a swipe of his paw.

'Oh!' Ellie laughed. 'That wasn't very nice! Will they fight?'

Charlie nodded. 'They'll have a few skirmishes. But they won't hurt one another badly. One of them will retire.'

'You think Hercules will win,' she said, and Charlie turned to her with a smile in his eyes.

'Yes. I've always thought so. He's an old campaigner. He understands strategy.'

Ellie gazed into Charlie's strong, handsome face, so close to her own, and suddenly wondered if that was what this was. Was Charlie playing a game of cat and mouse with her? If so, it was working. This morning, she wouldn't have consented to come out here with him. And here she was now, wishing he would kiss her again.

Of course, she wouldn't let him if he tried. But when he didn't try, merely turning back to watch Hercules playing near Jez, Ellie had to fight against an unwelcoming feeling of dismay.

It was comic to watch dear old Hercules. He would bump against Jez as though by accident, then walk away again. It was an altogether more subtle perform-

ance than Casanova's, and Ellie thought it was working. Jezebel was beginning to approach him.

'I think you're right,' she said, her tone a little
disgusted. 'I think he will win. By cunning.'

She heard Charlie laugh. 'A very important quality,
cunning. Unjustly condemned.' He turned to her once
more, his eyes lit with laughter, and Ellie knew at once
that he *was* going to kiss her, and that she wasn't going
to stop him at all.

The kiss was gentle but intimate, and it swept Ellie's
thoughts away. She returned it as she had the others,
caught helplessly by the emotion it aroused in her.

At the end of it, he looked down at her, smiling.
'Have dinner Thursday,' he said.

And Ellie nodded, somewhat hesitantly, but a nod it
definitely was.

CHAPTER NINE

'COME this way, Mrs Billings. Take a seat, and I'll soak that dressing off.'

Dulcie Billings obediently followed Ellie to the chair she'd indicated, and sat, propping her leg up on the stool. She'd barked her shin a week ago, and the skin had been too fragile and bloodless to suture, so it was a case of closing it with steri-strips and changing the dressing every few days. That was Ellie's task.

'Oh, it's doing well!' Ellie said when the pad lifted away. 'Only a few more days.'

The kind old lady smiled. 'I'll miss coming in and chatting to you, love. I'll have to see if I can bark the other shin.'

Ellie laughed. 'Oh, here comes Dr Carmody,' she said wickedly. 'He could probably do it for you!'

Charlie Carmody, hearing his name, came to stand over them, smiling down from his great height. 'What can I do?' he asked.

Ellie blushed and giggled. 'Bark Dulcie's other shin for her,' she said.

Charlie gave a great laugh. 'I probably could,' he agreed. 'You'd better steer clear of me, Dulcie. I'm in disgrace upstairs for tipping Sister's tea into her lap.'

Ellie chuckled as she applied the new dressing. She guessed his disgrace wasn't too terrible. Theatre Sister was one of those people in whose eyes Charlie could do little wrong.

He disappeared again shortly, and as Ellie said goodbye to Dulcie Simon Taverner materialised to take his place. As Ellie put the kidney bowl and dressing forceps into the steriliser in the sluice-room, he came to stand at her side.

'Have dinner with me tonight,' he said in an urgent voice.

Ellie shook her head. 'I can't, Simon. Even if I wanted to. I'm going out.'

He was silent for a moment, then he spoke in a tight, ardent voice. 'Then I'll have to say it here. Ellie! Ellie, I love you! Marry me!'

Ellie knew an urge to scream. Didn't she have problems enough? She slammed the door of the auto-clave, and for a moment leaned on the top. Then she turned to face him, and said with pain, 'I'm really sorry. I don't love you, Simon. I wish I could say it another way. But that's the truth. I just don't.'

For what seemed an eternity, Simon stood silent, his face pale and shocked. Then she saw his mouth give a twist, and he turned on his heel and left.

Ellie threw the dressings into the garbage, and wished she could crawl into a hole.

Charlie had said they would go to Bega. There was a good seafood restaurant there. Ellie had heard of it and knew it called for a dress. She had a jaunty little dinner number that was warm enough for the season. It was black velvet, with a straight skirt, coming to just above her knees. She pulled on sheer black tights with it and stepped into her shoes, then turned to the mirror on the wardrobe door to check the effect. It would do. Anyone else would have told her she looked wonderful, with her honey-gold hair against the black, and a figure that was made for a form-hugging velvet dress.

She was nervous. She didn't know what to expect.

She knew she probably shouldn't be going. What was Charlie planning to do now? What would he be like?

And when she walked self-consciously downstairs and found him waiting for her in the hall, none of her nervousness went away. He looked more like the Charlie of the mess dinner than of every day, tall and smashing in a well-cut dark sports coat and light grey trousers. But he smiled at her in the ordinary way and if he gave her the same sort of inspection that he had at the dinner he did it when Ellie wasn't aware.

It was Paul who came in as they were leaving and gave a whistle. '*Eh bien*, Ellie!' he said. 'That is very chic! Where are you going, you two?'

'To eat,' said Charlie prosaically, and it took some of Ellie's embarrassment away.

Neither did Paul make a big deal of it, merely saying, 'That is a good idea. The food here becomes worse, if that is possible.' But she would have been less comforted if she had seen him watching them drive off, and heard him say to himself with a smile, 'But excellent, Charlie! Go for it, *mon ami*!'

'Does it seem like a long way to drive to dinner?' Charlie asked.

'Oh, no!' said Ellie. 'Well, it is in miles, I suppose, compared to the city. But it doesn't take as long to drive to Bega as it took me to drive from my parents' place into the middle of Sydney to go to a show. And this is so much more pleasant. There it's bumper to bumper, crawling over the bridge in a jam that goes for miles.'

'Mmm. I don't think I'd like that,' said Charlie.

'I hate it!' declared Ellie. 'Though my mother writes that it's better now that the harbour tunnel has opened.'

'Where do your parents live?'

An so they passed the time quite comfortably chatting of Ellie's family till they reached the Bega speed-limit sign and finally drew up outside the restaurant. It was only when they were seated and Ellie faced Charlie across the table in candlelight that all her nervousness returned. For he looked undeniably wonderful like this. He rested his strong, smoothly shaven face on one hand and smiled at her with his fine grey eyes.

Ellie turned her own to the menu, lost for something to say. When they had ordered, however, Charlie took up the conversation again, easily talking of common things — of the hospital, the park, the people that they knew.

'How long have you been here, Charlie?' she asked curiously.

'Six years,' he said. 'Paul five. Simon two.'

'Will you stay here for good?'

'I think so,' he said placidly. 'I'm at home here.'

'Will the others, do you think?'

'Paul — possibly. Simon — no. I think he'll move on.'

'You'd miss Paul, wouldn't you?' she asked shyly, and he nodded.

'Yes, I'd be sorry to see Paul go.'

Ellie took a risk. 'But — not so much Simon?'

He smiled, a faintly rueful smile. 'No. Simon and I abrade one another.'

'I can't see that you abrade him,' she said frankly, but Charlie only smiled and said,

'Oh, yes, Ellie, I do.'

She gazed at him for a moment. 'Do you ever lose your temper?' she asked.

'I try not to,' he smiled.

'But do you?' she persisted.

'Occasionally,' he admitted.

'Somtimes I wish you would,' she said honestly. 'You just take it.'

He grinned. 'My mother says I was a placid baby.'

Ellie laughed. 'I can't imagine you being a baby, Charlie. What did you weigh?'

'Eleven pounds.'

Ellie grimaced.

'Yes, I think it was very nice of my mother to love me after that. I've felt guilty all my life.'

Ellie choked with laughter. He *was* a funny man at times. 'Is your mother alive, Charlie?'

He nodded. 'My father, too. Long-livers, the Carmodys.'

'Are you fond of them?'

He nodded again. 'Very.'

'What's your father like?' Ellie asked. 'Do you take after him?'

'No.' Charlie shook his head with a smile. 'I exasperate him. He calls me a lumbering ox.' It drew from Ellie another spurt of laughter. 'It really was better for Philip to stay on the property. He's less clumsy.'

'But you're very strong, Charlie. That must be useful.'

His eyes twinkled. 'Oh, yes. He'll grudgingly admit I come in handy at times.'

'Does he love you?'

'I believe he does.'

It had been a very personal question, she realised, and, though Charlie hadn't seemed to mind, Ellie felt her restraint return. Or perhaps it had been the way he had regarded her so steadily across the table, with that intimate warmth in his eyes. Ellie turned her attention for a while to her dinner, and was glad that he did the same. It wasn't until they'd reached the coffee that they re-established the same rapport. Then it was Charlie's doing

'What do you want in your life?' he asked.

'Oh, to nurse. To live somewhere like this — somewhere peaceful, with trees and open space.'

'Children?' he asked.

'Yes. Not too many. Two. Or three.'

'I can imagine that,' he said, and his mouth curved upwards. 'A little Ellie. With those eyes. And that smile. You look like an imp when you smile.'

Ellie couldn't help doing it, and covered her mouth with her hand. But he reached out and took it away, and kept it in his. She blushed, and tried to make her mouth prim.

'I like it when you try not to smile, too,' he said. 'I don't know which I like best.'

Ellie was all confusion. Her heart had speeded up. But he rescued her by saying, 'Shall we go?'

The night air was chill when they walked outside, but the car wasn't far away. 'This is the other thing I love about the country,' Ellie said. 'You can always find a park.'

'The thing I like is there are so few people in the street at night,' said Charlie, and with that he stopped dead, and swung her into his arms. She had a momentary glimpse of his grin before he bent his head and brought his lips to hers. She gave a little tremor of laughter, but it quickly fled as the passion in his kiss ignited hers. They clung there for a minute till footsteps made them part.

'Not that few,' said Ellie a trifle breathlessly. 'That was probably a patient.'

He opened the car door for her, saying with unimpaired cheerfulness, 'Probably. It'll be all over town by tomorrow.'

The memory of it lingered as they drove back to Berringar. Ellie wondered if it was meant to. He drove silently this time, and a couple of times took his hand off the wheel to stroke her own gently. It was amazing what a simple touch like that could do. If he wanted her to think about that kiss on the way home, and be longing for another, his plan was working well.

The common-room lights were out when they reached the Base. It was eleven-thirty. The crew had turned in. Only the new hospital building was well-lit, with Cas the brightest spot of all. Charlie switched the engine off as they stopped, but didn't get out of the car. Instead he reached out and drew her to him, and kissed her again. Ellie had been waiting for it for forty-five minutes, and it had all the force he could want it to have. The fire smouldering in her belly shot into flame.

'Charlie!' she cried at last, in panic at her loss of control.

He caught her face between his hands and whispered, 'What do you feel?' And when she didn't answer he repeated it patiently. 'Ellie, what do you feel?'

'I want you!' she almost sobbed, and he said,

'Trust that.'

He walked with her to the quarters, holding her arm, but he didn't pause at the common-room door as Ellie had thought he would. He put his arm around her shoulders and led her to his room. 'Don't fall over anything,' he said softly as he went to switch on a table-lamp. Its gentle light revealed a large room, part bedroom, part study, in considerable disarray. 'The lived-in look,' he grinned, and Ellie sat down on the bed and gave a rather hysterical laugh.

It was on the tip of her tongue to say, You need a wife, Charlie, but didn't in case he thought she was casting herself for the role. And then he had thrown off his coat and come to sit beside her on the bed.

Panic rose in her again. This man didn't love her. She didn't know how she felt about him. What was she doing here?

He didn't move towards her. She raised her eyes to him. He was watching her, his own eyes gentle and kind. 'You can walk out of that door any time you wish,' he said softly. 'Till you do, you can do whatever you want.' His beautiful mouth curved upwards and seemed to light his eyes. 'Is there anything you can think of that you'd like to do?'

Ellie gave a smothered laugh. He really was so nice! She sat smiling at him for a moment, then timidly reached out a hand and touched his lips.

'I think,' he said slowly, 'that means "Charlie, I'd like to kiss you again". Does it?'

Ellie nodded. His smile broadened. He said. 'Would you like me sitting up or lying down?'

Ellie gave another gust of laughter. 'Wh-what would you prefer?' she asked.

'Lying down. I'm inconveniently tall,' he said apologetically, and suited the deed to the word. He lay back, smiling up at her, making no move at all. And slowly Ellie bent over him, and brought her lips to his. It was exquisite to kiss him like this, and to feel his instant response. She was glad when he brought his arms up and lightly stroked her back.

'I like that furry dress,' he murmured against her lips, and she shook with another laugh.

'Velvet,' she said, moving her mouth a fraction away.

'Mmm,' he answered vaguely, finding it again.

It felt right—wonderfully right. And when they were lying full-length, pressed together, that felt right too. He was warm and so gentle, despite his great size. Ellie ran her hand down his side, delighting in the feel of him. And then he turned away from her, sat on the side of the bed and slowly peeled off his clothes.

He lay beside her again, stretched out before her gaze, and she thought she had never seen anything more beautiful or stirring in her life. He was lean-muscled, fit, powerful—a big man in perfect proportion.

Ellie drew a struggling breath and met his eyes. He smiled tenderly, and stroked her cheek with his hand. It was Ellie who reached out for him, who moved into his arms. Then Charlie held her, and kissed her, and at last undressed her, so that they lay there, gasping and trembling in each other's arms.

'Ellie, Ellie!' he whispered hoarsely, and rolled her away from him to make perfect love to her with his lips and his incomparable hands. And Ellie blazed beneath his touch like a flaming star, which flared out finally in the white heat of explosion.

And when the pieces of her seemed to float to earth and come together again, she found him leaning over her, his eyes locked on hers, a raging fire in their depths. His face was taut, a fine mist of perspiration on his skin. His breath was as rapid as if he had been running, and she felt him trembling against her. She had never seen passion as raw and powerful as this, and for a moment felt afraid of him as she never had before.

He drew a deep ragged breath, and said, 'What happens now is up to you.'

Ellie felt a flood of tenderness and admiration. This man, stretched as tight as a wire, was prepared to deny himself for her. She lifted her head and kissed the taut mouth, and whispered, 'I want you.'

He let out a shuddering breath, and covered her

body with his own, and then, to her surprise, joined himself so exquisitely gently to her that it didn't hurt her at all.

It was wonderful, beyond anything she had known. And Ellie watched his face as he had watchd hers. She thought she had never seen it look more beautiful than when he gave that great last rapturous groan.

They lay for a while on their sides, their bodies and eyes entwined, then Charlie eased himself from her, and wrapped her up in the covers as one would a precious child.

Ellie couldn't have said what time it was when she stirred, and Charlie responded by folding her more tightly and gently kissing her neck. But then she was suddenly wide awake again, drawn from sleep by the exquisite sensation of his warm nakedness. And she knew he was awake also, for she had felt his own swift, powerful response. But later all she knew was that some time in the enchanted night they made love again, this time more slowly. And Charlie possessed her and filled her till her desire mounted to a sweet agony and she blissfully dissolved in his fierce embrace. Only then did he yield to his own passion, and cry out hoarsely in its grip.

And afterwards, as Ellie lay against his heart, feeling it battering still against his chest, he whispered, 'Ellie, you're so lovely. You devastate me.'

Ellie felt a sweet stab of joy at the words. He wanted her. She gave him pleasure. For this moment, it was enough. 'You're beautiful, Charlie,' she whispered in return. 'It was so good!'

He held her tightly, and kissed her hair. 'Don't regret this, Ellie.'

'I won't,' she said. 'I couldn't.'

But he turned her face towards his own in the dark.

'Promise me, whatever happens in the future, you won't regret this.'

Ellie tried to imagine what might happen in the future, and knew a little nameless tug of fear. But she couldn't picture the future, so she said simply, 'I promise I'll try.'

In the morning she woke early, and turned to watch his peaceful sleeping face. But it wasn't long before he opened his eyes and gave her a contented, sleepy smile.

'What a lovely sight,' he murmured, then ran his hand over his chin with a rasping sound. 'I won't expect you to say the same,' he grinned.

She gave a soft laugh. 'You are a nice sight, Charlie. Even with a beard. I've never seen you like that before.' He did look different with his hair tousled and a night's growth on his face — less civilised, somehow, wilder. Ellie found it exciting. 'You look like a wild man,' she said.

He turned to her, smiling, a soft glint in his eys. 'I feel like a wild man,' he rumbled, and pulled her into his arms.

Ellie gave a giggle, then a gasp as their bodies met and she realised he was ready for her again. But he only kissed her, then gave a sigh and said, 'We'd better smuggle you upstairs.'

She glanced at the bedside clock and saw that he was right. The others would soon be up. 'You'd better wear my robe,' he decided, and climbed out of bed to get it. He stood before her holding it, and Ellie couldn't help raking the magnificent still aroused body with her eyes. She slid out of bed shyly, and quickly slipped her arms into it. But as she went to fold it about her he grabbed her by the lapels and, grinning, pulled her against him so that they stood naked, breast to breast.

'I always like to torture myself a little before break-fast,' he said, and Ellie gave a gusty laugh, which was stilled when he slowly traced the curve of her breast with his hand. Desire clutched again at her, but then he gave a stifled groan. 'That's enough,' he said a trifle breathlessly, and wrapped the gown around her. 'Go,' he smiled. 'Before I change my mind. Or lose it.'

Ellie tripped up the stairs in the gown that reached to her ankles and swallowed her hands. But she made it to her room unsighted, and sat on the bed, still clutching her bundle of clothes. It was a long time before her pulse settled down.

CHAPTER TEN

ELLIE had to muster her courage to go down to breakfast. She wasn't sure she could speak to Charlie in the company of others without somehow giving herself away. But when she got there she found she needn't have worried, for Charlie had been called straight to Cas.

The only circumstance to disconcert her was the presence of Simon, and he sat in silence. He didn't even glance at her until she spoke to Alison. Then, when she looked back in his direction she encountered his gaze, and Ellie saw his eyes harden and a light come into them that she didn't like. Dislike and anger seemed to shine out of them, and for a moment she felt oddly afraid. But in another second she saw him master himself and look away.

When Ellie reached Cas to take over from the night sister, a resuscitation was in full swing. A stockman had been bitten by a brown snake, and he was a sick man. Australia had the ten most lethal snakes in the world, and Ellie knew the brown snake was number two. But Charlie Carmody was moving fast as Ellie slid into the night sister's place at his side.

Someone had applied the only effective first aid — a constrictive bandage over the site of the bite on his leg. 'Don't take the bandage off,' said Charlie. 'The rest of the venom will move into the circulation. Just cut a hole in it over the bite, swab it and infiltrate adrenaline round the wound. That'll slow the absorption there.' As he spoke, he slid a drip into the man's arm. Ellie didn't know how he could find the vein and get the needle into it so effortlessly. The man's circulation had collapsed, and his veins with it. Ellie couldn't see any vessels at all. But Charlie had done it with one swift movement, and stood back for Ellie to connect the plastic tubing that would run in fluids and drugs. She taped it securely, and Charlie said, 'We'll sedate him now, and get in an endotracheal tube.'

Ellie could see that the man was fighting to breathe. The venom was paralysing his muscles, the respiratory muscles and diaphragm along with the rest. He was sweating and frothing at the mouth, and tears streamed involuntarily from his eyes. His heart-rate, displayed on the monitor, was a hundred and forty, and he constantly shook and twitched. Somehow, despite the paralysis, he continued to vomit. Ellie thought he must want more than anything to be put to sleep.

Charlie spoke to him calmly, his big hand on the man's shoulder. 'I'm going to put you out now, Ted.' He smiled into the man's eyes. 'This'll be over when I wake you up again.' Ellie thought she saw gratitude in Ted's eyes, along with the horror and pain.

Charlie shot the drugs into his vein, and followed swiftly with the tube into his windpipe as soon as Ted was inert. Ellie watched Charlie's hands as they performed task after task, moving deftly, surely, even delicately, and never still. She tried to anticipate what he wanted, to move in with the sucker at the right moment to clear Ted's mouth of saliva, to help secure the airway with tape.

'Adrenaline — ten mls, one in ten thousand,' said Charlie, and Ellie drew up the drug they would give the patient to stop him having a fatal reaction to the antivenom they would give him to neutralise the poison. 'Give it, Ellie,' he said quietly, 'then get the antivenom going. One ampoule in five hundred of saline. Got that blood sample, Peter?'

She did what he ordered quickly, and in a few more minutes Ted lay comatose, a tube down his throat, a machine breathing for him, antivenom and fluids running into his veins.

'A urinary catheter,' said Charlie, and Ellie scrambled to set up for it. Charlie worked calmly but with speed to install the thin rubber tubing in the man's bladder. The urine came out bloody. The venom had made the man's blood clot everywhere. He'd run out of clotting agent. Now he was bleeding through his kidneys. They would shut down if they didn't move fast. 'Get us fresh frozen plasma, Pete,' Charlie said. 'Ellie — a mannitol infusion.' The plasma would replace his clotting agents. The mannitol would keep up the flow of fluid through the kidneys.

They worked quietly on together, Ellie always aware of those strong, well-shaped hands. Seeing him now in this situation, calm and concentrated, totally in control, Ellie had trouble believing that only last night those same hands had worked their magic on her body, that this was the same man who had cried out with his passion as he'd lost himself in her.

Half an hour later the patient was wheeled out of Cas on a trolley, with ventilator and monitor either side of his head. Charlie walked beside him, holding up the bag of fresh frozen plasma flowing through the drip. Ellie turned as usual to the cleaning up, and once again her mind was free to return to Charlie Carmody. Her gut tightened each time she thought of last night. It had been exquisite. But what did it mean?

'You devastate me,' he had said, but not 'I love you'. There'd been no hint of that. And she herself — what did she feel? She liked him, admired him. She thrilled to his touch. But was this love? Ellie thought that if it was she would know. That was what everyone said. And she wouldn't have those doubts about him. For all his strength in the clinical situation, she still felt he was too gentle, too good-natured. She couldn't love a man she could push around.

Strange, then, that she could still feel a little stab of disappointment that he hadn't acknowledged her in any special way, even when he'd left to go to ICU. He had treated her exactly as he usually did, as though he'd forgotten their last embrace. And stranger still, when he returned in the afternoon and did make an intimate little gesture, that Ellie should feel such a glow of satisfaction.

She had not seen him come into Cas, but only became aware of his large figure looming beside her at the same moment that he ran his finger down the nape of her neck. She glanced up, feeling that now familiar clenching in her stomach, and received a warm, private smile.

'How is he?' she asked.

'Settled. Doing well.'

'I hope I never get bitten by a snake,' Ellie said devoutly, and felt his hand tense on her neck.

'Make sure you don't, Ellie,' he agreed. 'With your slim little body, we'd have a fight on our hands.'

She felt herself tremble, more from the intimacy with which he'd spoken than from fear of a snake. 'I don't suppose it'd bother you at all,' she said, her mouth turning up in that elfin smile.

He gave a rumbling laugh. 'No. You'd have to resuscitate the snake.' With that he looked swiftly round Cas, and dropped a kiss on her neck. 'I've got to go to Bega Hospital for a meeting. I won't be home till late.'

Ellie wanted suddenly to see him tonight. She wanted to say she would wait up for him. She found she couldn't. He might not want that.

But then he said, 'About eleven,' with a gleam in his eyes that told her she was wrong. He wanted to see her too.

With a tense, hot feeling in her belly, she said, 'I'll be up.'

After dinner, when she retired to the common-room beside the crackling fire, Ellie found herself reaching for the book of poems that Charlie had left on the table. Once again, she read her favourite, 'The Man from Snowy River', but now she seemed to hear Charlie's voice as she read. She finished the poem and sighed, and thought about it once again. It was a pity Charlie was so pliant. In every other way he was perfect, but that little spot of weakness, amiable as it no doubt was, spoiled him. He was a tractable giant, full of goodwill, who would let Simon mock and insult him without ever raising a protest. That Simon did his best to make Charlie a figure of fun made Ellie furious. There had been times when she herself had almost leapt to his defence.

Simon was absent, gone to the pub with some friends, so Ellie was able to relax completely, and it wasn't long before she fell asleep by the fire.

She awoke when a shadow fell across her. Her heart gave a glad leap, then she realised that it was not Charlie after all. It was Simon who stood over her, and swayed slightly in a way that told her he had had a lot to drink.

'Well, well. Sleeping Beauty,' he said in an unpleasant tone. 'What a lovely surprise!'

Ellie frowned. 'What do you want?' she asked rather sharply, her tone betraying her unease.

He didn't answer for a moment, and Ellie saw that his face was flushed, his mouth slack and the eyes over-bright. She amended her assessment. He was drunk as a skunk. 'How strange!' he said, slurring the sibilant. 'I could have sworn I'd told you.'

She opened her mouth to tell him he'd better go away, but he had leaned over her chair with a nauseating smell of whisky fumes and spoken first.

'I will tell you what it is, my love,' he said, enunciating carefully, but still slurring. 'I am going to help you discover your true feelings.' He gave a laugh which sounded reckless and discordant and which made Ellie shrink back into the chair.

'Like hell you are!' she snapped. 'Go away! You're disgustingly drunk and behaving stupidly!'

He laughed again. 'No, no! I was behaving stupidly before. I see what you need now. You need a firm hand.' He reached out and stroked her neck with a hand that shook, and Ellie flung it away.

'Just get this through your sodden brain, Simon,' she said through clenched teeth. 'You are not going to do anything!'

'But I am,' he said softly, and as he seized her arms Ellie saw the crazy feverish light in his eyes, half anger, half desire.

'Let me go!' she cried.

'Don't be frightened, my exotic flower. I can be as gentle as you allow me to be.' His voice was mocking and exultant. He had no doubt that he was going to have what he wanted, and that was because her own will was to be swept away.

'Get out!' she shouted, and it stirred him to action. He wrenched her out of the chair and pinned her with one arm to his chest, clamping his hand over her mouth.

'We can't have you making too much noise, my love,' he said. 'A few moans of pleasure we can allow.'

Ellie felt sick. She kicked and started to struggle, trying to bite his hand, but he was strong and wiry. He forced her backwards and her legs gave way when they came against the sofa. She fell across it with Simon's body on top of her. It knocked the breath out of her for a moment — long enough for Simon to grab one wrist and to force his knee between her legs. She tried to push him away with the other hand and to bring a knee up to fend him off. He grabbed her other wrist and brought his mouth down on hers.

She jerked her face away and sobbed in rage and fear and repugnance, but he had both wrists in one hand now and he wrenched her head back by her hair. She tried to scream but his mouth stopped it. She struggled harder as she felt his hand up under her skirt on her leg. Her heart was slamming. The smell of the drink and the feel of his mouth brought the bile to her throat.

She didn't hear the footsteps in the hall, or even when they swiftly crossed the room. She only felt Simon stiffen, and then his weight come off her as two hands picked him up and flung him against the wall.

She heard the thud as he hit it, and jerked herself upright to see Simon clutch at a shelf for support, and Charlie Carmody standing, fists clenched, immobile, close by. Ellie sobbed, and covered her mouth with her hand. Charlie didn't move. He stood like a tower, his knuckles white, his jaw tense, a look of black rage in his face that Ellie had never expected to see.

Simon straightened himself and clenched his hands into fists. Ellie thought he was going to launch himself at Charlie. But Charlie said, 'Don't make me kill you,' in a voice she barely recognised. Ellie saw the fear dawn in Simon's eyes.

Simon dropped his hands and took a step forward. 'Well, well, well,' he said. His voice was silkily sneering, but it shook just a little. 'Charlie. I wouldn't have thought it. So the little tart has you panting after her——'

He got no further. With a speed Ellie hadn't imagined, Charlie sprang forward, and a fist like a steamhammer smashed into Simon's face and sent him crashing to the floor.

He didn't get up. Ellie looked down to see him lying pale and rumpled where he had fallen, a welling pool of crimson gathering near his head.

Her eyes flew to Charlie in horror. He stood still, looking down at Simon, his face a frozen mask of rage. Ellie gasped. And suddenly fear clutched at her belly. Had he killed him? If so, he was a murderer! And they would put him in gaol! She knew in that instant that that was all that mattered — not Simon lying there dead on the floor. She gave a sob. 'Is he dead?' she croaked.

Charlie's face turned towards her and seemed to stare blindly for a moment, then slowly it relaxed and the eyes, as hard as granite, softened as they looked into her own. Another moment and his mouth had curved up faintly, and he looked a little like Charlie again. 'No,' he said at last. 'I didn't hit him that hard.'

And then she saw with a flood of relief that it was true, for Simon had stirred. 'Thank God!' she gasped, and buried her face in her hands.

'*Mon Dieu!*' Paul's voice came from the doorway, followed by quick steps across the room. He stood and looked from Charlie to Simon to Ellie, but only said, 'I will get a towel.' It was Paul who helped Simon into a

chair, and wiped the blood from his ashen face and
Paul who looked to see where the blood was coming
from. Finally he said, '*Morblue*, Charlie! You have
broken his jaw!'

Charlie spoke in a tone of cool indifference. 'I
thought I had.'

'Simon — hold this. You are able to hold this?' Simon
raised a trembling hand to the towel that Paul had
wrapped around his lower face.

'*Eh bien*, Charlie, what now?'

'Send him to Bega. They can fix him up there. He
can stay there. We'll have John Murphy instead.'
Charlie fixed hard eyes on Simon but he didn't make a
protest, and his own eyes slid away beneath the harsh
stare.

It was Paul who attempted to argue. He looked at
Ellie, then began to say, 'Charlie, don't you
think — ?'

But Charlie cut him off with one crushing syllable.
'No!'

Ellie was surprised. She had never heard that inflex-
ible note in his voice before. There was silence, then
Paul said, 'But Charlie — consider. . .' He glanced once
again at Ellie.

'I have considered,' came the uncompromising
answer. 'I've decided. He leaves.' Ellie searched the
face of this austere stranger, and felt a little shock at
what she saw. It was severe, with no sign of relaxation
at all in the strong square jaw. The grey eyes were
implacable. There was no way this man would give an
inch of ground.

Paul, who knew him well, also studied his face and
sighed. 'I see there is no point in arguing with you,
Charlie.'

'None at all,' said Charlie curtly. He turned to Ellie,

and his face softened again. 'I'm sorry,' he said. His tone was gentler, but Ellie wasn't fooled. She heard the resolve beneath it, and knew neither she nor anyone else could make him change his mind. Not that she wanted to. She would be glad if she never saw Simon Taverner again.

He turned to Simon and uttered one blighting sentence. 'If you ever behave like a drunken thug again, I'll break you in half.'

Ellie was glad when the ambulance came for Simon and took him away. Reaction had set in for her. Her teeth chattered. She stared dumbly at the pool of blood on the floor. She couldn't even cry now. The very horror of it stayed her tears.

Paul came back with a sponge and bucket. She watched him dully as he mopped the blood up and washed it out of the carpet. Then Charlie returned and she heard their voices in the kitchen. When they walked into the dining-room, she could hear what they said.

'*Parbleu*, I am glad that you hit him, Charlie, but I would also be glad if you didn't hit him so hard!'

'I didn't,' said Charlie.

There was silence for a second. Then Paul said, '*Bien*. Then do something for me, Charlie. Do not ever hit anyone hard.'

Finally Charlie came back to the common-room, and slowly lowered himself on to the sofa where Ellie still sat. For a long while he was silent. He did not touch her. Then tears finally came to Ellie. She covered her eyes with her hand and gave a rasping sob. She felt his hand press her shoulder and her name was spoken in a voice of pain. 'Ellie!'

'Charlie!' she cried, and he circled her quickly with

his arm and drew her to his chest. There, against his comforting strength, she quietly wept.

He stroked her hair. 'I'm sorry, Ellie,' he said softly. 'I'm sorry you had to see that.'

'Don't be sorry!' she gasped. 'Thank you!' She felt him tighten his clasp.

There was a long pause, then, 'You didn't appear to be enjoying his attentions,' he ventured quietly, and it made her give a gruff little laugh.

She looked up, and wiped her face. 'That was very acute of you, Charlie,' she said. And slowly her mouth turned up in a watery smile. 'What was it? The knee in the groin?'

The smile spread to him. 'That was part of it,' he acknowledged. 'I don't recall that I was forced to hold you by the wrists, or grab your hair.'

She gave a little giggle. 'You would have, of course, if you'd had to.'

'Certainly,' he agreed, and she gave a tremulous laugh, which turned suddenly breathless. For in that moment, for no reason she could have named, there came to Ellie the certainty she hadn't known before. In one crystal-clear instant, she knew beyond any doubt that she loved Charlie Carmody with all her body and mind and soul.

Her heart thudded as she lay against him. He must have noticed it, for he said quickly, 'Don't worry, Ellie! He won't do anything you don't want again.'

'I don't want anything from him! I don't want to see him!' she cried.

There was a silence, then Charlie said, 'Are you sure?'

'Yes!' she answered.

Then he said, 'Then you needn't. I can promise you he won't trouble you again.' Ellie heard once again the implacable note in his voice, and knew that he meant what he said. If Simon ever bothered her again, he would have to face a man built like a mountain, who could move when he wanted with the speed of a train. Somehow she didn't think she meant as much to Simon as that.

She opened her mouth to say, I'm glad you hit him! but didn't get a chance to utter the words. For Paul had appeared at a run in the doorway, still pulling on his clothes.

'Charlie — a head-on collision. They want us both in Cas!'

Ellie got to her feet with Charlie. 'I'll come too,' she said, but Charlie said,

'No!' in a tone that brooked no argument. 'You go to bed. If we're desperate we'll call you.' Ellie suddenly saw that for all his amiability there were times when you didn't debate with Charlie. This sounded like one of them.

'Yes, Charlie,' she said meekly, and did as he said.

CHAPTER ELEVEN

ELLIE awoke with a feeling of anticipation that reminded her of Christmas mornings when she was a child. It wasn't Christmas. It was a cold, crisp Saturday in June, and she was going to Goolcoola today to see Marian. But it wasn't that which filled her with suppressed excitement. It was the thought of Charlie Carmody, whom she knew at last, and loved.

Ellie sprang out of bed, and wiped the condensation off the window with her sleeve. Outside, everything sparkled with dew as fresh as the first day, with the first shafts of yellow light lying across the lawn. Dear, kind, tender, immovable Charlie! She laughed out loud. Had she really thought she would be able to push him around? One might as well try to move a mountain when he had made a decision he thought was right. How had she failed to see the steel in him?

She sighed as she felt a rush of emotion that was both tenderness and desire. Did he love her? He had made love to her with a mixture of gentleness and passion that exactly reflected his character as she knew it now. But he hadn't spoken of love. He had reacted to Simon's manhandling of her with almost murderous rage. Surely that meant something? He cared about her at least.

What of Marian? Ellie thought of her with a little frown on her brow. No. He couldn't love Marian. He *must* love her. For she loved him as much as it was possible to do.

The dew dried quickly from the lawn as Ellie ate

some toast in the kitchen. There was a pot of tea there, still lukewarm, that told her Paul and Charlie had had a long night. They must have only just now got to bed. She had told Charlie she was going to see Marian, and he had said, 'I'll come up if I can,' but it didn't seem very likely that he would make it now. He would need to sleep, and then there would be patients to see. Oh, well, she could do with a space for quiet reflection.

'Hi! How are you?' Marian came running from the ranger station, her dark face smiling. 'Didn't Charlie come with you? I thought he would.'

Ellie told her of Charlie's night, and that he was probably in a dead sleep.

'I don't know how you do that,' Marian said, shuddering. 'I feel sick at the sight of blood. I fainted last week when I cut my leg with the chain-saw.'

'Marian!'

'Oh, it was only a scratch,' she said quickly. 'I got my trouser leg caught in it cutting up some wood, and I took my finger off the trigger pretty quickly.'

'Marian, you could have cut your leg off!' Ellie said, appalled.

Marian made a rueful face. 'Oh, don't, Ellie! Tony's already told me — at three hundred decibels in language that blistered the paint on the walls. He's hardly spoken to me since.'

'Oh, dear. Is he still cross?'

Marian sighed. 'I've never seen him so angry. That was Tuesday. The only words I've heard from him since are ones like "imbecile".'

Ellie tried to repress a smile, but it was all right. Marian had given a choke of laughter too, though her eyes were sad.

'Oh, Marian. You see — he does care about you.'

'I don't think that's it, Ellie,' she answered. 'He said the sight of me plagues him.'

The two girls set off on the walk they had decided on, to a pinnacle of rock known as the Cathedral. It took two hours to get there, and the same back — a short walk, but Marian had to return to the station in the afternoon to help the other rangers relocate a wombat's lair. The wombat had chosen to make his home too close to the picnic area. He was attracting considerable attention from the visitors. Most people who came to national parks were sensible and conservation-minded. But there were exceptions and their initials could be seen carved in trees and scrawled on rocks. It only needed one of these people to stumble upon the animal. A marsupial resembling a small bear, he had no defences to speak of. He couldn't even see well, and his gait was lumbering and not very swift. Marian said they were going to find a more suitable spot for his burrow, where he might live out his blameless life in peace.

When they arrived back from their walk to help with the task, Ellie's heart gave a lurch to see that Charlie's car was there after all.

'They must have left already,' Marian said a trifle anxiously.

'You go on, then, Marian. I'll just dump my day pack in the car and catch you up.' Ellie wanted a few minutes to get herself together. The thought of seeing Charlie again, now that she was aware of her feelings, had made her pulse quicken and her chest tight. She tossed her pack on to the seat of the Suzuki, strolled across to the ranger station bathroom, then set off along the short trail to the picnic ground, her heart still beating quickly in anticipation.

How much a split-second in our lives could change

all we hoped and felt. For Ellie, such a malign split-second was only minutes away.

She found Tony and JB first. They had a wooden box with a hinged door not far from the wombat's burrow. It was baited with food, and they were setting a trail of titbits back to the wombat's hole.

'Good day, flower,' said JB, and Tony grunted. He didn't appear to be in the best of moods. 'Charlie's digging a hole over there. Marian's with him.'

Ellie decided to see where they'd chosen to put the wombat. She followed the direction of JB's pointing arm and set off through the trees, listening for their voices.

She didn't hear them, but she stumbled upon them anyway as she caught sight of Marian's green uniform through the bush. Her feet soundless on the carpet of leaves, she headed in their direction, then stood trans-fixed all at once as her view became clearer and she realised what she was seeing. In a place among the tall gums, Charlie's shovel lay idle on the ground. And Marian Brown was clasped in his arms. Charlie's cheek rested on the top of her head, and he was stroking her hair.

Ellie only watched for an instant — an instant in which all the colour seemed to drain from the world. Then she turned and stumbled blindly back in the direction she'd come. Her legs moved woodenly. She felt hollow. There seemed to be a stone where her heart had been. When she was halfway there she changed her mind again and struck off on a new course. She found a fallen log in the bush and sat on it, her mind numb with grief.

She tried to chide herself. It was only what she might have expected. She'd been warned by words and actions, and she'd been a fool to convince herself of

something else. Nothing helped. The tears welled up
in her unseeing eyes and her throat ached. They spilled
over at last and she sat by herself in the bush and cried
with bitter anguish.

He would be happy with Marian, she thought. She
deserved him. The thought gave her no comfort at all.
She was filled with an aching feeling of desolation. She
couldn't imagine finding another man like Charlie.
There couldn't be two such people in the world. And if
she couldn't have someone like him, she didn't want
anyone at all.

Ellie couldn't have said how long she sat there. She
knew that she couldn't stay there forever. They'd think
she'd got lost. She dragged herself to her feet at last,
and headed back towards the picnic area. Soon she
found what she was looking for — a little pool where
she could crouch and wash the tear-stains from her
face.

Charlie met her when she was almost back at the
picnic ground. 'Hello,' he said. 'We thought you'd
been snatched by a bunyip.'

He looked happy. Ellie's heart twisted inside her.
With a superhuman effort, she found her voice. 'I saw
a big goanna.' She found it was all she could say. She
brushed past him to walk back to the others, but he
reached out a hand and took her arm.

'Ellie? Is something wrong?'

She shook her head quickly, and forced heself to
encounter the keen grey eyes. 'Nothing,' she said, and
gave a quick smile that took away all her self-mastery.
'I want to see them move the wombat.'

He nodded and let her go, but there was a questioning look on his face.

The rangers had persuaded the wombat into the box.
Ellie was surprised to see how placidly he sat in it,

evidently waiting to see what would happen next. The men carried the box through the bush, and Ellie could see the wombat's myopic eyes peering through the slats. They put it down near the newly dug burrow, and Tony lifted the furry fellow out of his cage.

'Now, mate,' he said, 'you'll like your new house. It's bigger than the old one and it's full of carrots. And you'll find your old bedding in there too, so it'll smell like home.' He crouched at the entrance to the burrow, holding the docile wombat, and, placing him inside, gave him a little shove from behind.

The wombat turned and looked at Tony uncertainly, his furry ears pricked up. Then he turned towards the hole once more, sniffed once or twice, and waddled inside. They picked up the box and drew back from the entrance to wait and see what would happen. When he didn't reappear, Tony crept close again and listened. He returned to the group with a grin on his face.

'I hear the unmistakable crunching of carrots.'

The final job was to dig up the old burrow so that he wouldn't be tempted to return there. But Ellie didn't wait for that. She desperately needed some solitude. She offered to go back and make them some tea and sandwiches, and sprinted off along the track.

Their late lunch was a nightmare for Ellie. She poured tea, smiled, and tried to chat as though nothing had happened. Most of all she tried to avoid looking at Charlie's face. At four o'clock she felt she could respectably go, and bade them all a quick goodbye, only giving Marian a little hug.

'You'll come again, won't you?' Marian said.

'Oh, yes!' said Ellie, but she didn't see how she could. It would tear her heart out to see her friend being loved by Charlie. The only consolation was that, now they had come together, Charlie would naturally leave her alone.

'Ellie?' His voice made her drop her glass on the kitchen floor. 'I'm sorry,' he said as she picked it up. 'I didn't mean to startle you.'

'I—I wasn't expecting anyone.'

Charlie was silent as Ellie mopped up the water she had spilled. Then he said, 'What's wrong, Ellie?'

Damn him! Why couldn't he be vague today? He noticed too much. Ellie turned to the sink to refill the glass. 'Nothing, Charlie,' she said again.

She heard him approach and felt him take her elbow. 'That's not true,' he said quietly.

Ellie's heart ached at the touch. 'I don't feel like talking,' she said.

Gently he took the glass from her hand and swung her round to face him. His arms slid around her and drew her to his chest, but she stiffened and pulled herself away. 'What are you doing?' she said.

'Not talking,' Charlie answered, and gathered her to him again to bring his mouth down on hers.

Ellie felt an astonishment that momentarily stunned her. His mouth was moving on hers with the same passion that she'd felt before. She couldn't believe it. With growing anguish, she wrenched herself out of his arms. 'Don't!' she cried.

Charlie let her go, and stood there, searching her face.

Ellie turned to the sink and took a swallow of the water to hide the imminent tears. She still felt stunned. How could he want to kiss her now?

He watched her for a moment, then, 'What is it?' he asked.

Ellie couldn't speak. Helplessly, she shook her head.

'Is it what I did to Simon?' he asked softly, and again she gave her head a shake.

He really couldn't see any reason why he shouldn't kiss Marian one moment and her the next! Ellie took a deep breath, and said, 'I'm not like you.'

There was a pause, then he said, 'Go on.'

'I can't do it just because it feels good!' she blurted angrily. 'What—what kind of man are you anyway, Charlie?' Ellie rounded on him as she spoke, and let the tears stream down her face unheeded.

He looked at her with frowning concern, and finally shook his head. 'I don't understand you, Ellie. I don't understand what you're saying.'

'Well, how about this?' she cried. 'You're as big a bastard as Simon!' With that she threw her glass in the sink, and turned and ran away.

Ellie was glad she met no one on the stairs. She sat on her bed and thumped the pillow and cried. It wasn't true what she'd said. He was a bigger bastard than Simon. He didn't have any principles at all. He didn't care what he did as long as it felt good! 'If it feels right, it is right'—that was his selfish motto.

Ellie hurled the pillow across the room. Damn him! Damn him! And damn her for falling in love with him! He was just like his own animals—like Hercules or Casanova. He'd make love to whoever aroused him, like an animal. Like Neanderthal man!

Ellie didn't go down that night for dinner or coffee.

Paul asked, 'Ellie is out? Charlie?'

Charlie appeared to rouse himself from his reverie by the fire. 'Hmm? No,' he replied absently.

'She is sick?' Paul persisted. 'She did not come to dinner.'

'I don't think she's hungry,' Charlie said calmly, after consideration.

'Something is wrong,' Paul said, and Charlie nodded and made a noise of assent. '*Ma foi*, Charlie! I told you. You should not have sent Simon away.'

'She didn't seem to mind that last night,' he answered musingly.

'Last night! She was shocked. She has had time to think about it! She misses him.'

There was a long moment of contemplative silence. 'Perhaps,' he agreed at last.

'What are you going to do?'

'Think,' was Charlie's reply.

Paul Vassy made a sound very much like, 'Bah!'

Ellie didn't want to see Charlie. She lay in bed on Sunday morning till she felt sure he would be gone, and only then crept downstairs to go and make herself a cup of tea. But she found she had miscalculated. He hadn't left, though everyone else had. Once again they were alone. Ellie wrenched her eyes from him and walked quickly into the kitchen, praying that he'd stay where he was. He did so, and she forced herself to drink a cup of tea, sitting at the kitchen table where the domestics ate. Perhaps after what she'd said yesterday he was going to leave her alone.

But when she had drained the cup and set it down in the sink, she turned to find him watching her from the door. He was leaning against it, his big arms folded across his chest. There was a look of keen examination on his face such as he might give to one of his patients.

Ellie felt her heart give a painful squeeze. 'Go away, Charlie, please!' she heard herself say. There was only one way out of the kitchen, and he was standing there.

Charlie ignored it. 'Is that all you're going to have for breakfast?' he enquired quietly.

'I'm not hungry!' she replied.

'You didn't eat last night, either,' he pointed out with a calm that exasperated her.

'Who cares?' she cried childishly.

'I do,' he said, and it was all she could do to stop herself from rounding on him again with some bitter words. She couldn't do it. Morning had brought fresh counsel to Ellie. She saw that there was nothing she could blame him for. He had not lied. He had promised her nothing. It was her fault that she had dreamed of more than he could give. But it didn't stop her from being angry or hating him for the way he was.

'Have something to eat,' he said.

'Go away!' she said again. 'I'll eat when I want.'

'No,' he said tranquilly. 'You'll eat now, Ellie. You can't talk to me rationally when you're starving.'

'I don't want to talk to you at all!'

Charlie's voice sounded beside her. 'Possibly not,' he acknowledged gently, 'but you're going to do that, too.'

Ellie tried to side-step, but found herself clamped to his body by an arm whose strength made Simon feel like a weakling. It didn't hurt her, but it allowed no possibility of escape. 'Please ——' she began, but he hushed her. His voice was quiet and calm.

'I want you to sit down and eat a bowl of cereal. I'll get it for you. If I must, I'll do it one-handed. But I'll be less clumsy with two.' He waited, and Ellie realised how futile resistance was. He had the strength to make her do whatever he wanted and she could hear the note of finality in his voice. He seemed to read her capitulation from her body, and gently led her to a chair. She sat there, and soon he put a bowl before her on the kitchen table. He took the chair at her side.

'Eat it.' He still spoke quietly, but there was some quality in his words that made her unthinkingly pick up

the spoon. She ate half of it before she pushed it away,
feeling that if she had any more she'd be sick. He
didn't force her further, but only brought her a second
cup of tea. That she consumed more easily, and felt
slightly better when she put down the cup.

Then they sat in silence, Charlie's powerful form
sprawled in the chair beside her, his large hand resting
on the table. Finally he asked, 'Why am I a bastard?'

Ellie's face flamed with colour. After a time she said,
'You're not.' It was true. He had seduced her, but she
had been willing, and he had never deceived her.

A trace of dry humour sounded in his voice. 'Why
was I a bastard yesterday, then?' he asked softly.

She swallowed. 'You weren't.'

There was a pause, then, 'I wish you would explain
this to me, Ellie,' he said.

How could she? I love you, and you don't love me.
And I don't want to share you with Marian. And I
don't want to love a man who makes love to two
women at once. How could she say that? What could
she say that wouldn't result in her own humiliation?

'I can't. I only—made a mistake.'

Silence ensued again, then he said, 'Does this concern Simon?' She shook her head. 'Then what was the
mistake, Ellie?' He gripped her hand. 'Making love
with me?'

Ellie tried to pull her hand away, but he had it fast.
'Yes!' she gasped.

She felt him looking down into her face. 'It wasn't a
mistake for me,' he said in a low voice. 'But if you tell
me it was a mistake for you I must believe you. But
why deal with it this way? Why didn't you just tell me
you didn't want it again? It doesn't make sense. Did
you think I would force you?'

He was right. It wasn't an adequate explanation. She

couldn't think what else to say. Helplessly she shrugged, and found herself suddenly gripped hard by the shoulders, staring into his face, his eyes grown fierce. 'Did you?' he demanded.

She took a deep breath, shaken by his closeness and the look on his face.

'Did I force you before?' he asked. His voice dropped to an urgent whisper. 'Didn't you want to kiss me, and touch me, and look at me? Didn't you want me to fill you, and make you ——?'

'No!' she cried, and tried to wrench herself away, for desire for him had leapt up again, white-hot, at his passionate speech. 'Please, please,' she was sobbing now. 'Let me go! I know you didn't! I know you wouldn't! But I shouldn't have done it, and I don't want anything more!'

Still he held her fast, searching her face. 'Nothing?' he said at last.

'No! No!'

The grey eyes bored into hers. His face was taut, his breathing fast. 'Ellie!' he whispered. 'Not ——'

'Please, Charlie!' she cried in earnest, unable to take any more. 'Please, Charlie! Be kind! I can't say any more. I just want to be left alone!'

And suddenly, as his eyes swept over her tear-stained face, there came into his a look of pain. Perhaps it was concern for her distress, for he dropped his arms then, and didn't try to stop her when she rose and ran away.

CHAPTER TWELVE

MONDAY morning brought Bessie Lucknow back into Casualty. Ellie could see she was as bad as ever. She and Pete quickly did what was necessary, Pete not hesitating this time. He only called Charlie down when the ECG and chest X-ray had been done, and there was a line in her vein, the lasix and morphine and anginine already given. Charlie came down between theatre patients. He was going to be very busy for the next week, till John Murphy came from Bega to take Simon Taverner's place.

Bessie didn't look much better as yet. She was still gasping for breath. But she seemed to calm when Charlie came and took her hand, and she even managed a brave smile that wrung Ellie's heart.

'We'll take her up to Intensive Care,' Charlie said. 'I'll look after her there. Well done, Pete, Ellie.'

He was gone in another minute, and Ellie wondered through the day how Bessie was. She had looked worse somehow than the last time she had come in. At lunchtime, Ellie decided to duck up to ICU to find out.

She felt like a stranger there. She had only been upstairs a few times since she had come to the Base. Hesitating at the door, she saw that Charlie was there, in his natural habitat. There were four beds in ICU, three of them occupied today. It was a well-equipped and well-organised ward, a high-tech place where disastrous things could happen quickly and had to be as swiftly dealt with. Charlie was in his theatre pyjamas, sprawled in a chair behind the long two-tiered counter which was the control centre. His long legs were thrust out in front of him and his eyes were on one of the row of monitors. The ICU sister came and stood behind him, looking over his shoulder and leaning on the back of his chair with the ease of an old comrade. Ellie knew they had worked together since Charlie had taken over the Base. For a moment, she felt an irrational stab of jealousy at the obvious comfort and intimacy between them. She wondered if Charlie made love to Sister Warren as well. Perhaps he responded with primitive instinct to any attractive woman.

Sue Warren saw her and came to the door. 'Hello, Ellie. Did you want The Man?'

'No, I came to see how Bessie is. She didn't look too good downstairs.'

'She doesn't look too good upstairs,' Sister Warren said grimly. 'Come in. I'm just about to make *it* a cup of tea.' She indicated Charlie with her head. 'It's been as busy as a one-armed paper-hanger all morning. I'll be glad when Murphy comes. Do you want some tea?'

Ellie thanked her, but said no. She felt like an intruder.

But Sister Warren was friendly. 'Well, go and sit next to him. He'll tell you the worst about Bessie.'

Charlie looked up when she approached, and gave her a small smile.

'I wanted to see how Bessie was,' she explained hesitantly, feeling awkward. But he only nodded and pulled out the chair for her. Ellie's eyes went to the monitor he was watching. A succession of peaks marched across the green-lit screen, the electrical traces of someone's heartbeat. Now and then they became irregular, with runs of fast, abnormally shaped impulses.

'Is that Bessie?' she asked, and he nodded again.

'Runs of VT,' he told her.

Ellie knew what that meant. Ventricular tachycardia — abnormal electrical signals coming from the damaged ventricle of the heart instead of its usual pacemaker. It was often the precursor to a cardiac arrest.

'What are you going to do?' asked Ellie, and Charlie turned to look at her.

'I don't know,' he said in a low voice, and Ellie looked back at him in some surprise until he said, 'I've done tests on her heart this morning. It's barely moving, Ellie. So much of it's damaged now that if she survives this episode she'll be a cripple. She won't be able to walk. She won't have the strength or breath to do it. And she'll die within a few weeks in the same state you saw her in this morning.' He paused, and Ellie felt a vast sadness take hold of her, and a horror to think that Bessie was going to die in all the terror of suffocation. Then Charlie continued. 'Or, if I don't give her something to stop that abnormal rhythm, she may have a cardiac arrest. Her heart will stop, and she won't know a thing about it.' He turned his head and met her eyes again, and Ellie saw the pain in his. His voice was gruff as he said, 'What do you think she would want, Ellie?'

Ellie felt her heart go out to him for the terrible decision he had to make. Forgetting yesterday completely for the moment, she put her hand on his arm in a gesture of comfort. As absently, he put his hand over hers, and looked back at the monitor.

'Charlie——' Ellie tried to put her thoughts into words '—Bessie's a strong woman. She—she's always made her own decisions. I think you should ask her.'

Charlie gripped her hand more tightly. 'I know I should,' he breathed. 'Wise Ellie. I know I should.'

And slowly he withdrew his hand and rose to his feet. Ellie watched him go to sit beside Bessie Lucknow with her heart aching. She couldn't witness it. She knew she wouldn't have the strength to do it herself — to tell this lovely old lady that there was nothing more they could do, and to outline her choices. Feeling like a coward, she slipped out to tell Sue Warren that she'd have a cup of tea after all. She fould her unwrapping some sandwiches.

'Charlie's talking to Bessie,' Ellie said, and Sister Warren nodded.

'Good thing,' she said. 'Some patients don't want to know. But that's not one of them. And poor damn Charlie's got enough on his shoulders.'

'You've worked with him a long time, haven't you?' asked Ellie shyly.

'Five years. And I've seen him turn this hospital into one of the best of its type in the country. I've seen him do incredible work with the patients, prop up the staff, take over their work as well as his own when they're not coping. I've seen him so damn exhausted he could hardly stand up, and he still kept on giving.'

Ellie heard the note of maternal protectiveness in the older sister's voice. 'You look after him, don't you?' Ellie said, glancing at the lunch Sue was getting.

'Damn right I do. When the big ox'll let me.' She gave a brief grin, then became serious again. 'Nothing's too good for Charlie Carmody. If you'd seen what I have, you'd think so too.'

Ellie followed her back into ICU, carrying a mug of tea, and thought suddenly that Sue Warren was right. It was Charlie who carried the can around here. It was Charlie who held the Base together. Maybe he was entitled to take pleasure wherever he could.

Charlie and Bessie were sitting quietly now. Bessie

was holding his hand. Ellie could see that they had
finished their talk, and were just sitting together for
comfort.

'Have you got five minutes, Ellie?' asked Sue. 'Can
you sit with Bess while he eats?' Ellie agreed readily,
and went to take Charlie's place. 'Charles!' Sue called.
'Get over here! Drink this tea while it's hot.'

Charlie looked up and gave a little grin. 'That was
an order,' he said to Bessie. 'I don't dare disobey when
she calls me that.'

'No, love, you go and eat,' said Bessie kindly.
'You're fading away to a shadow.' A very substantial
shadow gave Ellie his chair with another sad little grin.

Ellie sat quietly by her, uncertain what to say. But
Bessie knew no such doubts. 'I never knew a better
man than Charlie Carmody, and I've been in this world
seventy-eight years.' Ellie wondered with some pain
whether she was condemned to hear Charlie's praises
sung by everyone she met today. 'Poor boy!' Bessie
continued. 'I knew anyway. I'm that glad he told me. I
don't want to go the way I was this morning. I've had
a good life, and I'm not scared, as long as it's nice and
quick.'

Ellie reached out a hand instinctively and felt
Bessie's grip hers. 'Don't you worry, love,' the old lady
said. 'And don't let him worry, either. He's got a loving
heart, like you. I don't want either of you feeling sad
about me. You think about each other.' The old lady's
eyes twinkled as Ellie blushed. She closed one eye in a
wink. 'I'm not too blind yet to see. He's got a light in
his eyes when he looks at you.'

Ellie was glad that she didn't have to tell the dear
old lady that that was lust. She merely flushed more
deeply and smiled. And soon Bessie was reminiscing
happily about the love of her own life, and Ellie could

hear that death held no fear for one who believed she was about to join him again.

Bessie Lucknow died while Ellie was there. She said she could fancy a cup of tea, and Sister Warren had taken Ellie's place as she drank it. Ellie sat beside Charlie again at the monitor, and silently drank the last of her own. She had got up to go when the monitor alarm went off at the same instant that the old lady's hand dropped limply at her side.

For a moment they all three froze as they fought inwardly against the ingrained patterns of thought and behaviour that an arrest alarm evoked. Charlie was the first to move. He leant forward and, with an abrupt movement, turned the alarm switch off. He and Ellie sat and watched the silent monitor as it displayed the dying flutters of that good, warm heart, till all they saw was a straight flat line. They stared at it for a while, then Charlie turned that off too.

Sue Warren got up with a sigh. She looked over at Charlie. 'Just as well, Charlie,' she said quietly, and he nodded, but didn't make a move. 'I'll go and get the certificates,' she said, and left the room.

Ellie swallowed, unsure of what to say, and aware of a lump in her throat. 'You knew her a long time, didn't you?' she asked.

'Mmm. She came in the first week I was here, and sent me some scones when she went home. I came to know her well. She was — a person who always wanted to give something back. She knitted me socks, and baked me cakes, and told me I was doing a good job.'

It touched Ellie's heart. She wondered if anyone else ever told Charlie he was doing a good job, or whether they just all loaded their troubles on to him. 'Charlie, you are doing a good job,' she said softly. 'You're doing a wonderful job.'

He looked down at her quickly, and made a move as though to embrace her. He would have checked it, but Ellie raised her arms to him, and in a moment they were hugging each other. Ellie was glad that they were largely hidden from the other patients by the counter.

'I'm sorry, Charlie,' she whispered.

'Thank you.' There was a pause, then he added, 'Ellie, I'm sorry for what I said to you. The way that I said it.'

Ellie shook her head. 'Don't be, Charlie. You were right. You said nothing but the truth. I wanted you.' The admission, made in a whisper, brought back all the feeling she had known in his arms before, and the memories of that wonderful night. She saw in her mind Charlie's beautiful body lying naked before her, and seemed to feel it locked with her own again. She felt his chest rising and falling, and his hands stir on her back.

'Was I wrong?' he asked softly. 'Was I wrong to make love to you?'

Once again she shook her head. 'No.'

'Do you regret it now? Do you feel badly about it?'

'No, Charlie.' Ellie was surprised to realise that it was true.

His hand tilted up her chin and she found herself looking into those grey eyes. 'You're not ashamed, Ellie? You're not ashamed of anything you did?'

She managed to answer, 'No, Charlie. I'll cherish the memory always.'

His arms tightened around her. 'So will I.' She felt his breath quick in her hair. 'But you don't want me now, Ellie?'

She knew it was a question, and searched for a way to answer that wouldn't mean telling a lie. 'Charlie, there has to be feeling for me. Not just physical feeling.

There has to be more.' She ached for Charlie to say, I do have feelings for you, Ellie. I love you.

But he didn't. He just held her for a long moment, then swallowed and said in almost a whisper, 'I understand.' When the door opened again, he let her go.

Ellie got up to let Sue Warren take her place beside him. She met his eyes once more, and received a sweet, sad smile that made her want all at once to reverse her decision, to fling her arms around him and kiss him and tell him he could have anything he wanted. She had to stop in the stairwell and wipe the tears from her eyes.

Ellie thought about the sadness in that smile for the rest of the afternoon. He had looked as though it really mattered to him. Or was it simply his sorrow about Bessie? Ellie felt a twinge of doubt about the validity of her own conclusions. But she thought about that scene in the park again, and found she couldn't reverse them. That had not been one of Charlie's friendly hugs he'd given Marian. He'd had both arms around her, and his cheek on her hair.

Work was the only balm for Ellie. It was a distraction and, to some extent, a solace. She was not at all sorry that they became very busy over the next week. The weather was cool but dry, with no rain for many weeks, and they had a succession of gusty sou'-westers which affected people's asthma.

Ellie saw Charlie every day, but they spoke only about the patients. If he had really felt sad about not pursuing their affair, he gave no further sign of it. He was as he had always been — cheerful and friendly, just perhaps more quiet with her. She tried to stop herself from watching him, and to stop her heart from lurching every time he walked into the room after an absence, but it was uphill work. Her eyes had a will of their

own, and would stray to him despite her efforts and
dwell with longing on his face and form. Once or twice
she had looked away quickly when he had turned his
head and caught her gaze.

Christine Rogers had come in again. She was a
twenty-year-old with severe asthma, and a history of
respiratory and cardiac arrests with it. This was her
second visit since Ellie had come. Last time Ellie had
learned that she came in every few months. This time
Ellie felt a thrill of fear when she saw her. It was bad.
Christine was sitting bolt upright on the ambulance
stretcher to facilitate what breathing she had. The
oxygen mask was on her, but she still looked bluish.
She was dragging breath in and forcing it out again
with all the strength at her command. Ellie could hear
the harsh wheeze from where she stood.

She and Pete flew to the stretcher, and Pete listened
with his stethoscope over her chest. His eyes sent a
signal to Ellie that she easily read. Christine wasn't
moving much air at all.

But the girl still had strength to gasp Charlie
Carmody's name. Ellie flicked her eyes up to Pete and
saw him nod in agreement. Ellie ran to the phone as
Pete prepared to put a cannula in Christine's vein.

Sue Warren swore softly when Ellie said that Charlie
was wanted urgently in Casualty, but when Ellie said,
'It's Christine Rogers—bad,' Sue said,

'OK. Wait. He's here.'

Breathlessly, Ellie told him the news, and he said,
'How bad?' more crisply than she'd heard him speak
before.

'Blue. Little air entry.'

'Tired?'

Ellie flicked her eyes to Christine, and said, 'Yes.
Exhausted.'

Charlie's voice returned like rapid fire. 'Set up for intubation there. Draw up Valium, ten mls, IV.' With that he dropped the phone.

Ellie flew down the ward and relayed his message to Pete. She slung the equipment for intubation together and drew up the Valium, meeting Christine's eyes briefly and saying, 'He'll be here, Christine,' with far more calm than she felt.

He was here, soon. Ellie had never seen him run before, but he was running when he arrived. He went straight to Christine and held her by the shoulders. A sort of joy leapt out of her eyes. 'Don't stop yet,' he said firmly. 'You can do it. Till I'm ready with the tube.'

Christine nodded, and continued to rasp in a little air with all the strength she had left. Charlie set the dials on the ventilator to the volume it would require to fill Christine's lungs, picked up the laryngoscope with which he would see down her throat to place the tube, and nodded to Ellie. 'Give the Valium.' Ellie shot it into the line in her vein.

Charlie watched his patient as the Valium took effect. Within a minute it had worked. Christine was out to it, and she wasn't breathing at all. In a few swift movements, Charlie dropped the bedhead down flat, extended her head and had the laryngoscope in place. Ellie slapped the tube into his hand the second he held it out. It was down Christine's throat and in her windpipe in two seconds, but Ellie was waiting with the hose to connect her to the ventilator. Charlie switched it on, glanced at the monitor which displayed her heartbeat, then shot a series of orders to Pete. Ventolin, cortisone, aminophylline — all the drugs that would keep her alive were assembled and given. In the next half-hour the pressure on the ventilator eased just a little, and a little more oxygen started to enter her lungs.

'Phew!' Pete said. 'Now I know what they mean by a quick intubation!'

Charlie looked up and grinned, but he added, 'That's about how long you've got, Pete, before her heart stops.'

'Then I hope she never comes in while you're not here, Charlie,' Pete said fervently.

But Charlie shook his head. 'You can do it, Pete.'

Peter looked as doubtful as Ellie felt.

Charlie went to phone Sister Warren, to tell her to transfer one of the ICU patients to the ward so that they had a bed for Christine. 'This'll take half an hour,' Charlie told Ellie as she came to fill out her admission forms. 'I'll stay here till Christine goes.'

Ellie was glad. She scribbled her notes, then, remembering what Sue Warren had said about his exhausting himself, made Charlie a cup of tea.

He looked up quickly as she put it in front of him, and said, 'Thank you.'

There was nothing for Ellie to do at the moment. Christine had arrived during one of the lulls that occurred from time to time. There was only one other patient, a boy with a fracture to his hand who had just returned from X-Ray and would now have the bone put in place and splinted by Pete. They didn't need Ellie's help—Vanessa was there. Ellie got up to draw the curtains between the boy's bed and Christine's, which was next to the desk where they sat. It screened Christine from anyone else's view but theirs, and screened the desk too, so that Charlie could drink his tea in peace.

Ellie put all Christine's notes together, made an entry in the 'Dangerous Drugs' book for the Valium, then leaned back in the chair. Charlie finished his tea, and got up to look at Christine. She watched him as he checked the gauge on the ventilator and the oximeter on her finger that was measuring the amount of oxygen in her blood. She saw the grey eyes sweep over the cardiac monitor and the machine that was automatically taking her blood-presure, and come to rest finally on his patient's face. He seemed to be satisfied, for he came and sat back down in his chair.

Once begun, it was hard for Ellie to stop watching him. She stole a look sideways at the strong profile and couldn't stop her eyes from continuing on over the beautiful male curves of him, right down to the muscular thighs. She flicked her eyes back to his face guiltily to make sure he wasn't looking, and found that he had turned his head and his eyes were staring intently into hers. Ellie's heart lurched and her face flamed, but he didn't take his eyes from her. Nor did he speak at once. When he did, it made her jerk her eyes up again from where they had sunk beneath that gaze.

'What are you doing, Ellie?' he asked slowly in a tense, low tone. His face was taut. 'If you don't want me, why do you look at me that way?'

It was unanswerable. She could only stare at him in dismay.

But he hadn't finished. 'I'm not insensate, Ellie. I see you looking at me. I see what's in your eyes.'

Ellie made a move as if to escape him, and he slid forward and pinned her with his arms. 'No!' he said in a harsh whisper. 'You tell me — what is it about? Look at me!'

Irresistibly, her eyes came up to his and met the full force of their clear grey. 'You do want me,' he said slowly. 'I see it in your eyes every day. It's there now,

Ellie. Am I wrong?' His voice dropped to a whisper. 'Tell me I'm wrong.'

She couldn't lie, not like this, with those penetrating eyes only inches away. She gave her head a shake.

'Don't look away!' he said, and she was forced to continue to endure that piercing gaze. 'What do you think that makes me feel?' he asked. 'What do you think I want to do?'

She couldn't answer. She could only keep looking, mesmerised by his eyes.

'I'll tell you. I feel I could behave like Simon. You said I was as big a bastard as he is. I feel I could be.'

She knew he was going to kiss her. Deliberately he moved his mouth towards hers. She gasped, 'No!' but he ignored her, and joined his lips to hers in a searing kiss. It all but made her swoon. Fire leapt up in her and melted her limbs. She couldn't resist him. She could do nothing but fight for air as the kiss took her breath away.

'Is that "no", Ellie?' he uttered fiercely as he took his mouth away. He kissed her again and again, pausing between each kiss to ask her, 'Is *that* "no"?'

Ellie felt trapped by her own emotions. She wanted to kiss him, to cling to him, to make love here where they sat. At the same time she longed, she needed to get away. A sort of panic rose within her, a feeling of desperation that suddenly made her cruel. She wrenched herself away from him, and dealt him a ringing slap.

She saw his face for a moment before tears blinded her eyes. She thought she would never forget it. It was pale, and frozen in a look of naked pain.

Ellie bolted into the sluice-room and slammed the door. She was not there to see the placid Charlie Carmody pick up his cup and hurl it at the wall.

Vanessa came to investigate the sound of smashing china, and stood looking from Dr Carmody to the shattered pieces on the floor.

'I dropped my cup,' he said in a hoarse voice. Vanessa looked at the six feet between him and the pieces, and gave him a long, bewildered stare.

CHAPTER THIRTEEN

ELLIE had regretted it the moment she had done it. Charlie hadn't deserved it. Once again he had said nothing that wasn't true. She had done it out of panic, out of anger at herself for responding to him, and out of anger at him for wanting her with his body but not his heart. She knew she must say she was sorry, but she couldn't face it yet.

John Murphy arrived that evening to take Simon Taverner's place. He was married and would live in town, but he and his wife had come to dinner at the quarters to meet some of the people he would be working with. John had wanted to work at the Base for a long time and was delighted to be there. He told them Simon was well again and had settled in at Bega. Ellie could tell that he was curious, and would have been pleased to know exactly what had happened, but no one filled him in. Charlie was friendly but rather abstracted. He answered John's questions, but fell silent again afterwards.

Ellie kept her eyes from him, and thought he was doing the same with her. But when dinner finished and he went out to feed the possums, she knew she must speak to him, however hard it was. She followed him outside and watched him as he emptied the feed into the enclosure, crouching beside the door. He looked up when she spoke.

'I'm sorry, Charlie,' she said simply. 'You didn't deserve that.'

He remained where he was, squatting on his heels

and looking up. 'Kind Ellie,' he said finally. 'I think I did.' And with that he turned to proffer some vegetable peelings through the little gate.

Was that all he was going to say? Did he want her to go away? Ellie couldn't do it. She wanted to offer him an explanation, the true one, cost her what it may. It was due to him now, after what she'd done.

'It's not true, Charlie. You didn't. You were right. Again. I—I panicked. I—was angry with myself for wanting you when I don't want to want you.'

She paused, but he didn't speak. Nor did he look around.

Ellie forced herself to go on. 'It's hard to tell you this. I don't know how to say it. You must leave me alone, Charlie, because——' She had steeled herself to say, Because I love you, and you don't love me, but he didn't let her finish.

'Don't, Ellie! Don't say any more!' There was pain in his voice. Slowly he stretched himself to his feet, but he didn't turn to her. 'What I've done is ill-judged and selfish. I know that. I don't want to cut up your peace, Ellie. I'm sorry.'

Ellie suddenly wondered if he already knew how she felt. His next words, uttered now, confirmed it.

'Feelings can't be forced. They're either there or they're not.'

He didn't have to tell her that. He didn't have to tell her that for him they weren't there. The blood rushed to Ellie's face. 'I know!' she said in a choked voice, and, to stop him saying more than could pain her, rushed on, 'I don't blame you for anything, Charlie. I understand, and I don't blame you.'

There was a pause, then he said with difficulty, 'It would be better if we kept our distance, Ellie.'

Ellie felt the final stab of humiliation in addition to

her grief. 'Yes. Of course,' she whispered, but she had
heard the note of grief in his voice. He was sorry for
hurting her, and she loved him too much not to offer
what comfort she could. 'It's all right, Charlie,' she
said. 'I'll be fine. Don't blame yourself.' With that she
turned and walked away too quickly to see him turn to
her with a sudden look of puzzlement in his face.

Only in her room did she let the tears roll unheeded
down her face. She thought she would hear those
words echoing forever in her brain. 'Feelings can't be
forced.' It was a gentle way of saying he knew she
loved him, and that he couldn't love her back. But it
hurt her as much as the cruellest, bluntest speech.

Ellie forced herself to eat her breakfast. She had to
return to some sort of normality. Life now had to go
on. Somehow she had to continue working with Charlie
Carmody as though there weren't a leaden weight in
her chest. He wasn't in the quarters. She had waited
till she was sure he would have gone on his Saturday
morning rounds. She thought that in any case he would
make sure he stayed out of her way now. He wasn't a
bad man. He had realised he was hurting her. She was
sure he would stop.

It surprised her, then, when she had finished staring
at the morning paper rather than reading it, to hear
him call her name. The colour surged into her face,
and she realised she would never see him now without
feeling embarrassed. But she put down the paper and
forced herself to look up. Charlie had come to stand at
the end of the table. He hesitated there, looking as
though he was unsure what he wanted to say, or
whether he wanted to say anything at all.

Ellie's heart sank. She didn't want to talk about it

any more. But perhaps it was about work. 'Yes, Charlie?' she said, wishing to get it over.

But he didn't answer. Instead he paced about the room, ruffling his hair with his hand. Finally he stopped in his original place, and looked at her with a frown. 'Ellie — forgive me. There's just one thing that you said last night that puzzled me.'

Ellie bent her head to her plate with a new wave of anguish. 'Charlie — I don't want to talk about it any more!'

It silenced him. But still he didn't leave. She stole a glance at him, and saw that he was staring into space with a distracted air. At last he turned to face her, and slowly shook his head. Ellie thought his face was curiously taut, the eyes turned to her revealing a burning intensity. When he spoke, it was almost grimly. 'I'm sorry, Ellie. It's too important. It's too damned important. I must know. I can't live with this doubt.'

Ellie stared at him, uncomprehending. What did he mean?

'It can't hurt any more than it does!' he said with a kind of agony, and for a dizzying moment Ellie felt that he was speaking not for her but for himself.

'Wh — what?' she stammered.

The grey eyes, normally so placid, bored into hers like lasers. 'Ellie, what did you mean when you said "I'll be fine"?'

What did he think she meant? What did he mean by asking her that? Ellie's mind whirled in confusion, and finally cleared to reveal to her the tiniest shaft of an agonising hope, penetrating her despair.

'I meant — I meant —' But Charlie Carmody was not destined to hear what she meant, as Ellie was not destined to reveal it. For rapid steps had sounded in the hall, and Paul Vassy's voice cut across their conversation like a knife.

'Charlie! Bushfire! A big one in the park! They want you!'

Ellie flew around in her chair, and saw that Paul had been running. There was an urgent look on his face.

'Tony saw it. On the north-west border in a gulley. It is spreading fast. There are farms. . .'

'All right.' Charlie's voice was calm. 'I'm coming.' He strode from the room.

Ellie tried to gather her thoughts when he had left. The news of the fire had banished all other considerations from her mind. The north-western border of the park. It had probably started from a day-tripper's fire. There *were* farms on the border there, but the farmers were careful of fire. It threatened their livelihood and sometimes their lives. She ran to the window to see which way the wind was blowing. It was from the south. So the fire would be burning at the moment towards the farms. If it dropped or veered, the flames would roar up the dry north-western slope like an express train and consume a large part of their beautiful park.

Ellie was frightened. She knew how few were their defences in this place against a fire. A few dozen men and two or three tankers were all that was available to them quickly. And quick their action had to be, or people could be hurt. She wondered suddenly whether she could do anything to help. Would they want a first-aid crew? Ellie didn't hesitate. She flew out of the quarters to seek Charlie and the others. She had an idea she would find them in Cas. They had a radio there.

As she ran she thought of Charlie. What would he do? Would he go out and help them fight the fire?

Would he take first-aid supplies out and act as doctor?
Would he be at risk? Would he be hurt? She couldn't
bear that, whether there was anything to justify that
crazy hope or not.

They *were* in Cas. A group of men was gathered
about Charlie — the leaders of the fire-fighting crew.
They were older men — tough, experienced bushmen.
They must have done this many times before. They
were all much older than Charlie, but somehow it
didn't surprise her at all to hear Charlie take command.

He was on the phone already. She could hear that
he was talking to Tony, in the park. Her eyes went to
his face — it was calm. A little remote even, as he
listened at the receiver.

'There's too much chance this wind will change,
Tony. It'll be a nor'-wester by mid-afternoon. I don't
like to spread our resources thin, but we've got to
cover both bases. We've got to defend both the park
and the farms. We need every available person. Get
Marian to stay on the phone and phone every person
around. Get the fire truck from Bateman's Bay up.
That makes four tankers — two in the park and two at
the farms. If the wind shifts quickly there won't be
time to re-deploy them. For the same reason, we need
to leave men in the park. It'll be hard for them to stand
by and do nothing while the others are fighting — but
the park is precious. I don't want to see it in ashes by
nightfall.'

His words, uttered so calmly, were chilling. Ellie felt
herself give a shiver, and her mind grasped little more
of what he was saying till he put the receiver down and
turned to the others. 'I'll go with you to Carson's farm.
If you agree, we'll divide the men evenly. Tony can
organise the ones in the park. There's no one better.
We'll send a first-aid crew to each place. I'll take a

nurse with me to Carson's. I'll send a doctor and another sister to the park. There are two ambulances on the way. We'll have them standing by as well.'

Ellie listened to the terse dialogue between the men. No one found fault with Charlie's plan. They were all grim-faced but calm and collected. Suddenly Ellie felt small and vulnerable. She knew she was trembling. What would they do without these men? She could never do herself what they were going to do.

But when they began to disperse she approached Charlie calmly enough and said, 'Charlie — do you want me?'

He looked at her for a moment, swiftly frowning. Then, 'Yes, Ellie. Thank you. I think we'll need you. Barbara's off duty too. I'll ask her to come with me. I'd like you to go to the park. With Peter.'

Ellie felt a pang of disappointment. She was afraid of the fire, but she had wanted to be with Charlie, where she could see that he was all right. It would be agony to wait in inactivity while he was elsewhere, perhaps in danger.

'Ellie — the wind will change. Unless we can control the fire down there, it will spread to the park. If that happens, I want you to go back to the ranger station with Marian. Any casualties can be brought to you there. Do you understand?'

She nodded dumbly. This was a Charlie whose word was law.

'Tony and JB have gone,' said Marian. 'They're down at the top of the ridge where the fire'll come if the wind turns.'

'There's a road into there, isn't there?' Ellie asked, and Marian nodded.

'Yes. Thank God, they can get men and tankers in there.'

'Can they get down the slope?'

'No,' said Marian. 'You can't fight a fire in dry bush on a north-western up-slope. It's the driest side of the hill, because of the afternoon sun on it. And heat rises. Have you seen a bushfire up close?'

Ellie shook her head, but was able to imagine something of it from the haunted look in Marian's eyes.

'They'll have to let it burn up the hillside and then try and stop it on the ridge.'

'Do you think the wind will change?' asked Ellie anxiously.

Marian nodded. 'Charlie says so.' It seemed enough for her. 'There's a tanker!' she said, and ducked outside to give the driver detailed directions.

Even though the wind was in the opposite direction, it wasn't strong, and by lunchtime Ellie could smell the fire in the air. Peter had already joined the waiting men, but there was nothing to do there, and Ellie had stayed at the ranger station to help Marian make sandwiches. Finally they loaded up the jeep with food and drink and prepared to take it to the top of the ridge.

As they drove north-westwards, the smell of the fire was stronger, and the bush was oddly silent. All the birds had fled a danger they'd already sensed. Ellie tried not to think of the animals, especially those like koalas and wombats, who were slow and not very good at fleeing from fire. Despite her best efforts, her thoughts turned to the wombat they'd relocated. She prayed that if the fire reached him he'd stay in his burrow, and not get frightened and try to run away.

But then she forgot him as they reached the last ridge and caught a glimpse out over the boundary of the park. Ellie gave a gasp of shock and horror. They could see the fire now below them, burning on a half-mile front in the bush on the edge of a farm.

'Oh, God!' groaned Ellie. There were flames from the ground to the treetops — a slowly advancing wall of fierce red fire whose blood-chilling roar could be plainly heard from here.

She saw Marian's hands grip the steering-wheel whitely, but the ranger said nothing, and soon they came to the men. Ellie saw Peter, sitting on the back bumper of the ambulance with the driver. They'd already organised the first-aid supplies they'd brought from the Base.

The men were glad to see the girls with food for them. It was hard for them to stand there immobile and watch their colleagues fighting the fire.

'Good on you, precious,' said JB to Marian, and helped her unload the sandwiches from the car.

'JB, how are they going?' asked Ellie anxiously, and he turned to give her a wink.

'It's all right, flower,' he said. 'Charlie's got 'em organised. They're going pretty good considering they've only got two tankers and they're fighting it mostly with sacks.'

Ellie knew what he meant. There'd be a line of fire-fighters, each trying to beat back the blaze in the undergrowth with wet hessian bags.

'But it's in the treetops, JB!' she said.

'Yeah,' he conceded. 'But Charlie will be using his tankers and hoses as well as he can. He's fought fires before, flower. He knows what he's doing. And he's got some good blokes with him.'

Most of the men assembled here were farming people from the southern side of the park. They stood about talking in their slow country accents, their cattlemen's hats worn low on their foreheads, shading their eyes.

'Carson'll be lucky,' said one of them lugubriously. 'It's getting there.'

'Yeah, but very slowly,' said another, 'an' it's twelve-thirty already. Carmody's right — the wind'll change. They don't 'ave to stop it. They just 'ave to slow it down like they're doing.'

'Charlie down there?' asked a third man. 'Wondered where 'e was. They'll be right, then.'

There was a murmur of general assent which made Ellie feel oddly proud. She had to remind herself that it was a slim hope indeed that the man who had won the confidence of these hard-bitten farmers would ever be hers. Lord knew what he had really been going to say.

Ellie heard Tony's voice behind them. 'Brown, what are you doing here?' he sounded annoyed.

'We brought up some lunch,' she told him.

'Yeah, all right. Good. Now get back to the station.' His tone brooked no argument. Ellie and Marian made their way to the car.

'I wish it would rain,' said Marian in a wistful voice.

'I wish it would deluge,' said Ellie, 'and hail and snow.'

Marian managed a little chuckle. 'And before the fire gets up that ridge.'

'I hope Charlie's all right,' said Ellie anxiously, speaking her thoughts, and then blushed as she remembered to whom she was speaking.

But Marian answered quite calmly. 'He's very competent, Ellie. He was born in the country. Charlie's been fighting fires all his life. We had one down the road last Christmas and Charlie was everywhere at once and thinking ten steps ahead.' She paused, then continued. 'You don't realise at first, with Charlie. You think for a while he's—well, a bit of a klutz. But he's anything but, you know.'

'Yes, I know,' said Ellie softly, and wondered when Marian had discovered that, and how long it had taken for her to fall in love with him afterwards.

'Of course,' said Marian apologetically, 'you must know better than I do.'

Ellie nodded. 'He's a superb doctor.'

Marian sighed. 'He's such a nice person, too.' Then she stunned Ellie momentarily by saying in a wistful voice, 'I wish Tony were just a *bit* more like him.'

Ellie's heart was in her mouth as she asked, 'Do you—still feel the same about Tony?'

Marian sighed again, and said, 'I'm a hopeless case, Ellie,' and Ellie felt herself go limp.

Then what had happened in that clearing? Marian hadn't pushed Charlie away. What was it all about? Ellie wanted more than anything in the world to ask. But she didn't have it in her. All she knew was that the shaft of hope had just widened a little and, slim though it still was, it seemed to light her soul.

By two o'clock the southerly wind had petered out. The air was still and deathly, heavy now with the fire's smoke. Already cinders were drifting down around the station. The women realised that the fire must be burning up the hill.

'Ellie, I don't care what Tony says—I'm going to see.'

Ellie didn't hesitate. 'I'm coming with you.'

Now, on the trip to the ridge-top, Ellie did see wildlife. It was in evidence everywhere, moving from the path of the blaze. By the time they were halfway along the road, the air was thick with smoke and cinders, and already making them cough. She wondered aloud how they could fight a fire in this atmosphere.

'Yeah. It's better in a way if there is some breeze,' said Marian. 'Then at least they're not so likely to choke to death.'

But there was some breeze by the time they reached the ridge-top. It was Charlie's nor'-wester just beginning to fan the fire from behind. Ellie opened her eyes at the scene of destruction. They knew there would be no reprieve now, and the men had been cutting a fire-break in the bush. They were there sitll, working feverishly with chain-saws and axes, felling the timber and hacking the undergrowth out.

'They need more men!' said Marian, looking down the hillside. The flames were close now, and burning still on a front of perhaps five hundred metres. 'I'm staying, Ellie. You take the truck back.'

Ellie seeing the task that faced them, swallowed and shook her head. 'I'm staying, too.'

The man at the truck they approached didn't spurn them. In answer to Marian's question as to what they could do, he handed her an axe, and thrust into Ellie's hand a bush-knife the size of a machete. 'Down there.' He pointed. 'Cut down the undergrowth.' He realised that this was no time to consign the women to the kitchen. They needed every pair of hands they could get.

As Ellie hacked at the bushes, she thought of Charlie. She wondered where he was now. Was he on his way back? Carson's farm was all right, she heard. The fire had turned back on itself with the wind change. It would burn itself out down there. Now it was the park which stood in its path.

It began to be hot. Ellie wanted to take her long-sleeved shirt off. But she knew enough about fires to know that you should keep your skin covered. She straightened up and peered down the hillside. She saw all at once the reason for the temperature. The fire was racing towards them. The hair on the back of her neck stood up. She listened. The sound was different now. It was a constant menacing growl, like the thundering roar of a speeding train.

She heard men calling over the noise — they were all to retreat to the ridge-top. They'd done as much as they could.

Neither Ellie nor Marian thought of leaving. Marian grabbed a wet sack, like the men. Ellie knew she must go and wait with Peter. She couldn't help anyone else if she was hurt.

'Good God!' Peter looked appalled when he saw her. 'What are you doing here? Go back to the station! Charlie will tear me limb from limb if he finds you here! He told me to make sure you went back!'

Ellie gave him the best grin she could manage. 'I'll tell him you tried, Pete.'

Pete groaned. 'Great!' he said. 'He'll put me in hospital.' He then added mournfully, 'Probably that little ward in the basement.'

'What's that?' Ellie asked.

'The morgue,' said Pete so lugubriously that Ellie had to laugh.

They stood a hundred yards to the rear and waited, watching the line of men strung out along the ridge. Ellie pulled up the mask Pete had given her. Already her eyes were streaming, and she could feel the smoke at the back of her throat. It must be much worse where Marian was. Her eyes sought her friend, and she was glad to see that someone had given her a mask too.

And then the fire had reached the fire-break, and

the mind couldn't deal with anything else. Face to face with that crackling, spitting, roaring inferno, Ellie was suddenly cold. A shout went up. She dimly heard it. She saw the men and Marian move forward together to pit themselves against the flames.

The next hour passed in a kind of daze. It was like some scene from hell, only more full of noise, Ellie was sure. The sound was battering, brain-numbing. She couldn't hear the shout of the others — just the incessant terrible roar of the blaze.

There seemed to be fire everywhere, leaping across the fire-break. The fighters turned to each outbreak doggedly and beat at it with their sacks. The tankers were pumping as hard as they could, directing their four hoses into the trees, over the fire-fighters' heads. It wasn't long before there were casualties — men overcome by smoke despite the partial protection of their masks, one with cinders in his eyes, a burnt leg, some temporarily overwhelmed by the heat. Ellie and Pete and the ambulance driver worked rapidly. A few minutes of oxygen, the eyes irrigated with saline and drops instilled, ice-packs and dressing to the burns, and one by one they struggled to their feet again and went back to the line.

After a time, Ellie worked automatically. She no longer felt afraid. She went to give help wherever it was needed, even crouching beside a patient on the charred ground at the very front of the blaze. Pete had given up telling her to stay back with the ambulance. Her mind slipped into remote control, dulled by the swirling smoke and that everlasting noise. There was no sense of time, no thought any more — just a sensation of searing heat and overwhelming chaos.

* * *

On the north-west road two tankers and a convoy of
fire-fighters raced towards the park. Charlie Carmody,
blackened and sweat-stained, drove calmly, though not
at his usual laconic pace. Paul Vassy would have had
nothing to complain of today.

'I hope they've got that fire-break cut,' said the
equally blackened man at Charlie's side.

Charlie nodded. 'They'll have done it.'

At last they turned in through the park gates, and
pulled up outside the ranger station.

'No activity here,' said Barbara from the back seat.
'Maybe they haven't had any casualties.'

'Hopefully not,' said Charlie. 'They'll have had the
minor stuff that Pete and Ted can patch up quickly. It
doesn't look as though they've had to bring any out to
Ellie. You stay with her, though, Barbara. It could
happen any time.'

Barbara grabbed her first-aid box, and slid out of the
vehicle, calling, 'Take care,' as she slammed the door,
and Charlie drove on towards the fire.

Ellie saw the burning branch fall from the tree on to
the man next to Marian. She had been up at Marian's
end of the line attending to someone else. A gasp tore
from her as she saw him pinned to the ground by it.
But it was only seconds before his mates and Marian
had kicked it off him with their boots. Ellie was there
in seconds too, glad that she was carrying oxygen. She
placed the mask on his face in place of his smoke mask
and turned it on, then inspected the damage. He was
burnt on the chest and upper arms, across which the
branch had fallen, his clothing stuck to him. She didn't
think there was anything broken. But he was definitely
out of the line — their first major casualty.

'Can you carry him back?' she asked the men. 'He's

OK, but he'll have to be evacuated.' She caught sight of Marian as the men hoisted him and began to walk back towards the ambulance, and noticed that her friend was trembling with fatigue, her face livid beneath the black of the smoke. Ellie thought quickly. 'Marian, will you go with them and carry the oxygen cylinder, please? I haven't finished here.' She would check on the man she'd treated before. He was dehydrated, and she had left him a little back from the blaze swallowing electrolyte solution. Then she would speed back to the ambulance and make sure that Marian stayed there.

Ellie glanced back, with a little shudder, at where the tree branch had felled the fire-fighter, then realied that they'd left his smoke mask on the ground. She darted back and bent to pick it up, and all at once heard a mighty 'whoosh' behind her. She didn't realise at first what had happened. But when she looked up and seemed to see fire all around her, she suddenly knew, and the fear that had left her earlier returned with a sickening violence she'd never known before. She turned one way and another, her heart pounding, her limbs feeling limp. The flames had jumped the fire-break, high in the treetops above her head, and spread to the timber on her side of it. Now a wall of flames reared up in front of her and behind her. There didn't appear to be any way out.

CHAPTER FOURTEEN

'THEY'RE doing well!' exclaimed Charlie's companion. 'We'll win, Charlie. With two more tankers, and men. . .'

They piled out of the truck and ran across the road. Tony ran towards them, and for a minute they shouted above the noise.

The tankers arrived, and Charlie gave them orders. More men appeared and reported to Charlie to be directed.

It was then that Charlie saw Marian. She was running towards him, her dirt-streaked face dead white. He ran to meet her.

'Charlie! Charlie! It's Ellie!' She was half crying. 'She's cut off! They can't get to her! We saw it happen!'

For a split-second she saw on his face a look of starkest horror, then he was racing in the direction from which she'd come.

Every second seemed to Ellie to last forever. Her mind was numb. At first she couldn't think at all. Then what she'd been taught came back to her: If all else fails, get down low and cover yourself with anything you can. She dropped to the charred ground, her knees almost giving way as she bent them. The voices of her education were right. There was less smoke down here. And she still had her mask on.

But there was nothing to cover her—only the dirt on the ground. She could feel by the searing heat around her that it was not enough. If she stayed here she had

minutes and that was all. She stared at the wall of flame
before her. You must run through the flames, the
voices in her head said. Run—run like the wind. If
you're fast enough, you'll survive. She swallowed con-
vulsively in her horror. Then she sobbed aloud, 'I
can't! I can't!'

Charlie reached the men beating at the flames behind
Ellie, their white, desperate faces showing what they
thought of their chances of success.

'Get away!' cried Charlie. 'You can't do it! Get the
tanker!'

One of them dropped his sack and ran to do as
Charlie said.

Charlie whirled round on Marian. She was sobbing
openly now. 'Which way?' he rasped, and she pointed
towards the blaze. He turned to the man whose job
was to wet the sacking. 'Douse me!' he commanded,
and the man didn't argue. He emptied his bucket over
Charlie, filled it again and dumped a second lot over
the big man's head and shoulders, reaching up to do it.

Marian stared at Charlie, at his set jaw and fierce
eyes, not understanding at first. Then her own eyes
opened wide with horror as she realised what he
intended to do.

But he didn't look back at her, or say another word.
He pulled on his mask, then turned and ran like a
charging bull straight into the flames.

Ellie was crouching, her eyes half blind and streaming,
staring at the wall of fire. The world was full of swirling
smoke and the heat seemed to press on her like a
weight. She thought she must take her mask off. It
would be better to die from the smoke than to be burnt
to death. With trembling fingers, she tore it off her,

and it was only half a minute before things seemed to fade and darken. I'm going to die of the smoke, she thought, and felt glad. Then she only knew she was falling, and nothing more at all.

She wasn't aware of the next few minutes. She didn't feel the strong arms that plucked her from the ground. She didn't know the searing heat as those arms bore her through the wall of fire. It was only after they'd put the oxygen mask on her that she awoke enough to realise she wasn't dead. Then she found herself gazing up at a blackened giant of a man whose face beneath the soot was as pale as death itself.

She could feel that she was soaking, and that she seemed to be packed in ice. The man leaning over her was dripping on to her. She opened her mouth to try and speak, but found she could only cough and gasp. She felt his huge hand grip her arm, almost painfully, and heard the deep welcome resonance of his voice.

'Don't talk,' he commanded. 'Just breathe on the mask.'

Marian rode with her friend in the ambulance, and saw her wheeled into Casualty. They were separated then for a while. Dr Murphy put a drip in Ellie, and examined her when Vanessa had undressed her. Much of her skin was reddened, as though she'd been sunburned, but there wasn't a serious burn on her. She might peel in places, but that was all. There'd be no scars. A chest X-ray came next, and John Murphy came back to tell her that it was satisfactory. They would do another one tomorrow, to make sure that the smoke hadn't injured her lungs. They would give her fluids overnight. She could probably go back to the quarters tomorrow.

When Marian saw her again, she was lying comfortably in a bed, her skin clean now, and dressed in a clean white hospital gown. The oxygen mask was still on her face, but she could talk.

'I'm all right,' she said. 'But I have to stay overnight and have another chest X-ray in the morning.'

Marian gave a smile of relief. She slid thankfully into the chair beside Ellie's bed. Ellie saw that Marian's trouser leg had been half cut off and that her leg was bandaged. Marian saw her look at it.

'I was too slow,' she said cheerfully. 'It's not a bad burn.'

Ellie knew suddenly how she'd got it. She'd been trying to get to her. Tears brimmed all at once in Ellie's smoke-reddened eyes. The faithful face of her friend swam before her. 'Thanks, Marian,' she croaked.

Marian looked embarrassed. 'Thank Charlie,' she recommended.

Ellie's eyes rested on Marian's, a frown in them as though she was trying to remember. 'I don't know what happened,' she said at last.

'He got you,' said Marian simply. 'He ran through the fire.' Despite her efforts not to show it, something of the horror of that moment appeared in her eyes, and Ellie saw it.

Her face paled. She didn't speak. Then, 'Oh, God!' she whispered. 'Marian—he—he's all right?' It was a plea.

Marian nodded. 'Of course he is. We're talking about Charlie. He's fine.'

'But—but is he burnt?'

Marian hesitated. 'His shirt caught a bit, but the men were waiting with buckets. I think maybe his arms were a bit burnt, but they didn't look bad, Ellie. Maybe his face. . .where the mask didn't cover it. But not bad. He was so fast, you see. He was like a charging rhino.

Nothing could have stopped him.' She grinned at Ellie finally.

Ellie tried to return it, but the tears had welled up once more and overflowed. 'I wanted to do that — to run through the fire. I didn't have the courage.'

'I don't blame you!' said Marian emphatically.

More tears followed their brethren over Ellie's pink cheeks. 'Maybe I shouldn't have been there.'

Marian shook her head decidedly. 'It wasn't your fault, Ellie. All the men said that. The fire jumped the gap up in the treetops. The men said you worked like a Trojan.'

Ellie gave a little sob. 'I wish I could see Charlie,' she said. 'Just to know he's all right. Even if he's angry. He told me to stay at the station if the fire came. I disobeyed him. Oh, Marian — tell me the truth, if he's badly burnt! It's all my fault!'

'Ellie, honest! I wouldn't lie! He's OK. Charlie's indestructible!'

Ellie managed a watery smile; but she knew she couldn't rest till she'd seen him.

'Where is she?' they heard a male voice say, and Ellie turned her head expectantly, but realised in the same moment that it wasn't Charlie. The voice belonged to Tony. And in a second he stood before them, a remarkable sight with his skin and clothes black, his hair singed and his red eyes fierce. He looked from one to the other, subjecting them both to a long, silent inspection.

Finally he spoke, in a voice made hoarse by smoke and shouting, and perhaps by emotion. 'They told me one of you girls had been taken to hospital. I thought, Nah, you're wrong. I distinctly told Brown they were both to stay at the station.'

Marian bit her lip as Tony stood, silent again, taking

in the details of Ellie's oxygen and Marian's bandage. She shrank a little as he took one step towards her.

'Brown — you tell me! What do I have to do to keep you out of trouble?'

Marian had no answer. She stood immobile, gazing at him helplessly, waiting for his rage to break over her.

He made a noise of exasperation. And in a moment he had stunned them both by stepping forward and jerking her roughly into his arms, where he pressed her fiercely to his chest, his grasp so firm she could scarcely breathe.

He stood still and silent, his eyes closed tightly as though in pain. When he spoke at last his voice was more gruff than ever. 'You're a stupid, disobedient, obstinate, useless female!' he said. 'You'd better marry me. You can't look after yourself.'

Ellie saw, over his shoulder, a look of purest joy and wonder spread over Marian's face.

Ellie couldn't help smiling to herself after they'd gone. It was just the sort of proposal Tony would make, she decided. And as she recalled as well the radiant happiness she'd seen on the face of her friend she reflected that the form of it really didn't matter.

She had asked him about Charlie as soon as it seemed tactful to do so. Tony had said, 'Don't get the vapours, Standish, he's all right,' in answer to her anxious question, and the look of shrewd scrutiny that had accompanied his statement had made her drop the subject.

The fire was under control, Tony had said. They'd beaten it back behind the fire-break. It was burning itself out now. But he thought Charlie would stay with the men tonight and make sure things stayed that way.

He was wrong. At half-past eight that night, Ellie awoke from an uneasy doze to find Charlie standing beside her. Her heart gave one great, painful lurch, and her eyes raked him. But he was standing there, as big and solid as usual, and smiling gently. Ellie couldn't help it — a single sob escaped her, and she covered her face with her hands.

She felt him lower his bulk on to her bed and heard his deep voice, calm and gentle. 'I regret to tell you, miss, you're a very bad patient. Keep that drip arm still!'

She moved her hands and looked up quickly to see that he was grinning. And despite everything it drew a tiny chuckle from her in return. But her smile soon faded . Charlie was clean now, his face no longer black. But the skin on his forehead was red and in places blistered, and his forearms were bandaged.

Suddenly Ellie knew that if she spoke she would cry in earnest. He might have comprehended, for he gazed at her a moment, then took her hand in his great big paw and gently stroked her arm. The clear grey eyes smiled down into hers.

She managed a few syllables at last. 'I'm sorry! I didn't do what you said.'

The smile curved his mouth again. 'No,' he said softly. 'I'll wait till you're well. Then I'll beat you.'

Ellie's heart speeded up at the tenderness of the tone. Her green eyes scanned his face. 'Aren't you angry?' she asked, and saw his face become serious.

'No,' he said briefly. 'No room for that.'

'But your arms!' she said in a choked voice. 'Your poor arms! And your forehead!'

'Shh!' he said. 'Nothing. Only blistered. Won't even scar. And I've still got eyebrows, remarkably enough.'

She knew he meant her to laugh, but she couldn't.

Another sob escaped her. 'I wanted to run through it. I knew I should. I wasn't brave enough. . .' Her voice trailed away in a tone of anguish as she remembered those few minutes of hell.

Charlie moved swiftly, sliding forward and taking her in his arms. He held her lightly against his chest, and gently stroked her hair. 'Shh!' he whispered again. 'It's over now. All over. Don't think about it any more.' But she thought there was a note of agony in his voice, too, as he repeated, 'Don't think about it!'

'Charlie! Thank you!' she sobbed.

But he only gripped her a little tighter and said, 'Don't! No need! Don't talk any more now. It's time you went to sleep.'

'But——'

He moved back from her and gave a half-smile, but his voice was firm as he said, 'Ellie Standish—just do one thing I've asked you to do today.'

She gave a shamefaced little laugh and said, 'OK.'

'Lie back. Close your eyes,' he commanded.

Ellie did it, her hand still in Charlie's. She wasn't aware of it when later, with infinite weariness, he rose to go away.

'Right-o. I've got the boss's permission to give you the flick!' Caroline said in the morning.

Ellie smiled. 'X-ray all right?'

'Yep. How did you sleep last night? Noisy place to try and sleep, Casualty. Even with the curtains pulled round.'

'I slept like a corpse, Caroline! I didn't hear a thing. How's the chap the branch fell on?'

'Roy Grainger?' said Caroline, who knew everyone in the district. 'He's good. Charlie told me when I dressed his arms just now.'

'How are they, Caro? Charlie's arms?'

Caroline made a face. 'Blistered,' she said. 'But OK. No deeper burns. They'll be fine. Must be painful, though.'

'He saved my life, Caro.'

Caroline smiled down at her. 'Yeah. Well, that's our Charlie,' she said, adding archly, 'No doubt he thought it'd be too much trouble recruiting another cas sister.'

'Must be it,' said Ellie with a little smile.

'Yeah!' said Caroline in a disbelieving tone that made Ellie turn away, blushing, to don her clothes.

There was a smell of smoke in the air still, but Ellie hardly noticed it as she walked slowly back to the quarters. Her mind was too busy. Caroline thought Charlie cared for her, but she didn't understand. She wondered whether he knew now about Marian and Tony, and how it had affected him. Did he have a broken heart? She couldn't be really glad about Marian and Tony if that was the case.

There were so many questions still without answers. Did Charlie love Marian? Why had Marian let him hold her in the bush? What had he meant yesterday? And why had he risked his life for her?

But no—there was no mystery there. The Charlie Carmody she knew would have done the same for any of them. She must be careful not to read too much into that. All at once, Ellie was angry with herself. She was weaving a fairy-tale. He had desired her, but not once had he spoken of love. It was Marian he'd spoken of with fondness, and, even if he couldn't have Marian, that didn't mean he would ever love her.

'How do you feel?' Charlie's voice made her start. He had come into the quarters behind her, and followed her into the kitchen where she had gone for a drink.

'Like I was at a hell of a party last night,' Ellie said with a little smile.

He laughed, and the beautiful sound of it made her throat feel tight.

'How do *you* feel?' she asked, and he answered, 'About the same.'

'Your arms and face must hurt,' she said painfully, but he only shook his head and smiled.

'I've got something to show you,' he said.

She looked at him enquiringly, but he only smiled again and held out his hand. Shyly she gave him hers, and he gently led her to the door and out to the possum's enclosure, where he stood with one hand on her shoulder till she realised what it was he had wanted her to see.

'Charlie!' she cried in surprise and delight. Two possums were curled up together in the treehouse Charlie had made. Charlie stooped and picked up a stick and tossed it. It fell with a rattle on the roof. The possums put their heads up — the female and Hercules, the old man.

'It's Hercules!' she cried. 'Charlie! Have they——?'

Charlie grinned down at her. 'Yes.'

Ellie laughed. 'That's wonderful!' she exclaimed, then added thoughtfully, 'Then she chose Hercules after all! You always thought she would.'

Charlie looked down at her, smiling. 'Yes, she was dazzled for a while by the young one. But she's really a wise little animal. Her choice in the end was made on sound evolutionary grounds. She chose the less pretty but stronger one, the one with the scars to show he can fight and stay alive.'

Ellie watched them settle down again. 'A happy ending,' she said in a voice that came out a little wistfully. She felt Charlie's hand tighten on her shoulder.

'Charlie——' she began, and Charlie answered quickly,

'Yes, Ellie.'

She paused to find the words. 'You said last night not to thank you. But that's ridiculous. You risked your life for me!'

'No,' he said gruffly. 'Only my eyebrows.'

Ellie gave a choke, then burst out laughing, unable to help herself. She looked up at him and encountered a broad grin. 'Oh, Charlie! You are unique!' But in a moment she became serious again, her eyes steady on his handsome face. 'Charlie — I don't know how to thank you. If it hadn't been for what you did, I'd be dead now. I don't know how you could be so brave.'

Ellie saw a strange light enter his eyes and his smile became oddly twisted. 'Not brave,' he said hoarsely. 'Desperate.'

Ellie stared at him, not trusting herself to interpret his meaning, but with her heart hammering all at once against her ribs. She swallowed with difficulty. 'I don't understand you,' she whispered.

His eyes gazed with razor-edged keenness into her. 'Don't you?' he asked. 'Is it possible?' A note of anguish invaded his voice. 'Is it possible that I've stuffed things up so badly that you don't know I love you desperately?'

Ellie felt joy explode in her with an intensity that brought tears to her eyes. But she could only stand and nod.

He gave a strangled groan, and clutched her to his breast. 'Ellie — is it — do you——?'

'I love you, Charlie! I love you!' she breathed, and then he was all but crushing the life from her and kissing her in a way that left her trembling and breathless. When he'd finished, he looked down at her, and Ellie saw all she wanted to see in his eyes.

'Oh, Charlie! I thought you loved Marian! I—I saw you holding her in the bush!'

Comprehension dawned in his face. 'All the things I thought of! But I never thought of that. Paul's right. I *am* an imbecile!'

Ellie gave a choke of laughter, but still he looked rueful.

'I'm very fond of Marian,' he said. 'Tony was awful that day. The way he was actually made *me* feel there was some hope for them. But it didn't affect Marian that way.'

'Charlie, were you *comforting* her?' she asked.

'Trying to,' he replied gruffly.

'Oh, Charlie! I think *I'm* the imbecile!'

And suddenly they were laughing together, till Charlie suddenly said, 'How could you think that, when we——?' He looked at her in pain.

Ellie regarded him steadily. 'You never said you loved me, Charlie,' she said in a whisper.

Charlie's voice was low and tight. 'You cared for Simon. I didn't think you'd want to hear that from me. But I knew you responded to me physically. I thought in time it might come to be more if I didn't frighten you away.'

'Charlie, I never cared for Simon. He drove me crazy! I liked him at first, as a friend. But soon it wasn't even that. I wanted him to leave me alone, but he wouldn't!'

Charlie looked at her with a face that was comical in its dismay, then pulled her hard against him. 'Oh, God!' he groaned. 'I should be put down!'

Ellie found herself giggling, till he said in the same tight voice, 'Ellie, do you think you could bring yourself to marry an imbecile?'

She hugged him as hard as she could, and whispered, 'I couldn't marry anyone else,' and for a while speech wasn't possible as their lips met again in a kiss.

When it was over, she saw Charlie's mouth turn up in a tender, rueful smile. 'The first time I kissed you was impulse. I couldn't help it. But when Simon came back from Bega that night, I knew he'd never make you happy, whatever you felt. I was determined to win you from him any way I could. I didn't think you'd thought of loving me, but I knew you liked me, and that you were attracted to me physically. I decided to work with what I had. I set out to seduce you, Ellie,' he confessed.

'I know, Charlie,' she said with a little smile. 'You did it awfully well.'

A momentary look of surprise was slowly supplanted by a heart-warming grin. 'Considering I've been so stupid, it's conceited of me, isn't it, to think I'm the correct Darwinian choice?'

She gave a gurgle of laughter. 'You and Hercules have a lot in common.'

He seemed to find it a compliment, for he pulled her to him and kissed her again. When he had finished, the tender warmth in his eyes had given way to a burning look of aching intensity. 'I love you so much,' he muttered hoarsely, and crushed her to his chest.

'Oh, Charlie, I love you,' she whispered, and was rewarded by a tightening of his massive arms that threatened her very existence. 'Charlie — when did you know?'

He looked down at her face. 'When you caught my cup, and grinned like a little imp,' he said 'When did you?'

'When you hit Simon,' she said, with the very smile he loved.

He grinned back. 'Then I'm damn glad I did!'

'So am I!' declared Ellie.

'Ellie, do you mind a mate who's a trifle absent-minded?' he asked. With shining eyes, she shook her head. 'And clumsy?' he added apologetically.

Ellie looked up at him, at the tender, passionate light in his eyes and the smile on his beautiful mouth. 'No. I love it,' she said truthfully.

'Then say you'll marry me,' he whispered.

Ellie answered, 'I will!' She nestled against him for a moment, savouring the joy of being held against that wonderful, powerful body, in the circle of his sheltering arms. Then she looked up at him suddenly, and gave him the most impish grin. 'I'll marry you, Charlie,' she said. 'And I've got a great idea. We'll ask all the wedding guests to give us a kettle!'

Paul Vassy, emerging from the quarters in quest of Charlie, was brought up short by the sight of his colleagues kissing and laughing at the same time. A smile dawned on his face and he stood there, contentedly watching them. '*Eh bien*, Charlie,' he said softly. 'Well done.'

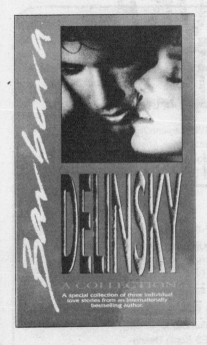

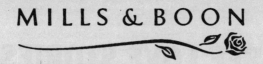

MILLS & BOON

LOVE ON CALL

The books for enjoyment this month are:

NOTHING LEFT TO GIVE Caroline Anderson
HIS SHELTERING ARMS Judith Ansell
CALMER WATERS Abigail Gordon
STRICTLY PROFESSIONAL Laura MacDonald

♥   ♥   ♥   ♥   ♥

Treats in store!

Watch next month for the following absorbing stories:

LAKESIDE HOSPITAL Margaret Barker
A FATHER'S LOVE Lilian Darcy
PASSIONATE ENEMIES Sonia Deane
BURNOUT Mary Hawkins